MW00613902

Showdown at Comanche Butte

(Remington Series 3)

by

Robert Vaughan

Print Edition
© Copyright 2016 Robert Vaughan

Wolfpack Publishing
P.O. Box 620427
Las Vegas, NV 89162

All rights reserved. No part of this book may be reproduced by any means without the prior written consent of the publisher, other than brief quotes for reviews.

ISBN: 978-1-62918-513-2

Chapter 1

AS THE SUN ROSE over the buttes to the west, Tom Blue, a Comanche Indian, and six of those who had chosen to follow his renegade ways, stood just below the crest of a ridge, looking down on the ranch below. Tom Blue told himself and those who followed him that he had taken to the warpath because of such places as this ranch.

The white man's government had moved the Five Civilized Tribes from the Eastern United States into what was now called Indian Territory. It made no difference to the white man's government that the Comanche, Kiowa, Cheyenne and Arapaho Indians already lived there. They were simply moved west, into the short grass country. Now the white men were coming here, and they were coming in ever increasing numbers. They came with plows to rip open the land and with cows to eat the grass of the buffalo.

Tom Blue told his followers that this was the reason he had gone the way of the renegade, defying not only the white men but the council of his own tribe. It made a good rallying cry, but it wasn't true. Tom Blue was a renegade because he enjoyed it. He liked the whiskey he could get for the money and goods he stole...and he liked the terror he caused when the white men heard his name. But most of all, he liked to kill.

"Look," one of those with Tom Blue said, and Tom Blue looked in the direction indicated. He saw three men come out of the house and begin their morning chores. He smelled the smoke of the breakfast fire, and he heard the woman inside the house call to the children. One of the men of the ranch went into the small house the whites used for their toilet, and it was while he was in there that the two men Tom Blue had sent as decoys started their false attack. They fired their rifles and let out blood-curdling screams, and Tom Blue smiled, for they made as much noise as three war parties.

"My God! Where the hell did they come from?" one of the whites shouted, and he started for the house. "Belle! Injuns! Injun attack!"

The man's call was shut off by the whistle and thunk of an arrow. It was a shot of nearly fifty yards, and when the bowman saw he was successful, he let out a victory yelp.

The man who had been in the outhouse came out then, with his pants down around his ankles. He hopped around, trying to pull them up, but three arrows struck him. The third man tried to run away, but at a signal from Tom Blue, two warriors chased him down, then killed him with bone-crushing blows from their war clubs.

With the three men dead, the Comanches began moving toward the ranch, moving with less caution now, for only the woman and children remained.

Suddenly and unexpectedly, a shot rang out and one of the Indians went down with a bullet in his chest and a look of stark surprise on his face. The other Comanches scrambled for cover. They looked toward the house to determine from which window the shot had come. They couldn't tell, so one of the Indians, in a show of courage, stood up and ran from one position to another. He shouted to attract the woman's attention, hoping to draw her fire.

But no shots were fired.

Another warrior tried the same tactic as the first, but he too was unsuccessful. The woman simply did not fire.

Finally, moving one at a time, the entire raiding party advanced to the house; then, emboldened by the fact that not one shot had been fired at them since the first few shots, Tom Blue kicked in the door and leaped into the house. What he saw there surprised him, for there, sitting up against the wall, were two little girls and a grown woman. Tom Blue watched in shock as the woman shot each of the little girls, then put the barrel of the pistol in her mouth and pulled the trigger. Blood and brains splashed on the wall as the bullet smashed out through the back of her head.

Two of his followers, Billy Blackhat and Rufus Coyote, burst into the room behind him, ready to do battle. They stopped short when they saw what had happened. The woman was sitting there with her eyes still open, but with her head twisted at a grotesque angle. Blood and brain tissue ran down the back of her head, soaking the yoke of her dress.

"Why did she do that?" Billy Blackhat asked in surprise.

"Because," Tom Blue spat. "A white woman would rather die than let an Indian have her."

"Ha! That is only because I have not had a white woman," Billy Blackhat said, cupping his crotch and laughing. "If a white woman knew me, she would kill herself before letting a white man have her again."

The others laughed at Billy Blackhat's ribald joke, then each of them in turn told of their own prowess with women.

The woman who shot herself had long yellow hair, and Tom Blue felt angry, as if she had cheated him. He spat at her, then kicked her. Around her neck dangled a cameo brooch of ivory, suspended from a tiny gold chain. He jerked it off.

"Well, we should not let the breakfast go to waste, should we?" Rufus Coyote asked, and he reached for a pan of biscuits. The pan was sitting on top of the stove and consequently was still hot, so Rufus Coyote burned his fingers. He let out a yelp of pain and stuck his fingers in his mouth, quickly. The others laughed, then they too began poking through the kitchen to find something to eat.

"Will you eat?" Billy Blackhat asked Tom Blue.

"No," Tom Blue answered.

Tom Blue walked out onto the front porch of the ranch house and stood there with his hand on one of the roof support posts. Behind him he could hear his men laughing and talking and reliving the "battle," though Tom Blue knew there was very little real fighting this morning.

"What a shot!" the bowman who had killed the man with a single arrow said. "Never has there been a warrior who could kill with a bow from such a distance."

"Listen to him," Rufus Coyote laughed. "Soon he would have us believe he is the greatest bowman to ever live."

"Tom Blue! Look!" Billy Blackhat shouted, running onto the porch with an armful of rifles. "There are four rifles here, and many, many bullets. What luck we have had! I'm going back to see what else I can find."

Tom Blue stayed on the front porch and listened to the conversation of his men. He thought of what had happened here this morning. It was the sign of a good leader to win a victory with very little fighting, for that showed that he was a good tactician and able to outsmart his enemy. But he didn't know how much longer he would be able to continue with no opposition. So far the army at Fort Supply had stayed out of it. The white trader who gave him whiskey in exchange for the goods he stole had told him that the army would not come after him.

"They're afraid it might start a whole war iffen they was to send the army after just a few Comanches," he explained. "Ye' ain't got nothin' to worry about from them."

The whiskey trader might be right about the army, Tom Blue thought. But he wondered about the U.S. Marshals. Tom Blue rubbed the scar on his cheek and thought about one of them. He had had a run-in with a U.S. Marshal about two years ago. He had pulled his knife on the marshal, thinking he could frighten him off. The marshal wasn't frightened off, and the scar on Tom Blue's face had come from his own knife. The marshal's name was Remington. Tom Blue had remembered it well. If the Marshal came for him again, he would be ready for him.

"Most of it is worthless junk," the trader told Tom Blue a couple of days later when he and the others came into the trading post with booty taken from his raid.

"Is this not worth much?" Tom Blue asked, showing him the cameo brooch of ivory he had taken from the neck of the woman.

"Sure, if we was in St. Louis or Cincinnati it might be worth somethin'. Out here there ain't nobody gonna pay anythin' for it. What else ye' got?"

"Some cattle."

The trader smiled. "Ah, now, there's somethin' I can use. Ye' bring me cattle an' I'll always have somethin' for ye'. The cattle I can take up to Kansas an' sell. Yes, cattle is good. Here's some whiskey now. Take it with my blessin's. An' anytime ye' get the chance to get more cattle, go ahead an' take it."

"I don't like cattle," Tom Blue said. "Cattle eat the grass of the buffalo."

"Well, then, ye' see, ye' can do a good deed for yer people by bringin' the cattle to me, then. I'll take it up to Kansas an' get it outta here so we leave the grass for the buffalo."

"I will find more cattle," Tom Blue promised.

After the War Between the States, John Duncan and Linus Rawlings left Georgia and the broken lives and lost cause behind them. They moved to Texas, where they married girls who were sisters, thus making them brothers-in-law as well as friends.

They had. been farmers in Georgia, but in Texas they went on a cow hunt, rounding up wild longhorns until they were able to start a small ranch of their own. Drought, winter storms, disease, and other problems plagued them year after year, but this year, for the first time, they had over a hundred head of cattle to drive to market, and the price at the railhead in Kansas was twenty-five dollars a head. At long last the ranch was about to pay off.

John Duncan couldn't recall when he had been so tired. It was a bone-aching, back-breaking tired, and yet there was an exhilaration too that transcended the tiredness. The exhilaration came from the excitement of the drive and from the feeling of accomplishing some good, hard work. John wasn't the only one affected by the excitement of what they were doing. He could see it in the eyes and on the face of Linus as well. The excitement was infectious and self-feeding and it seemed to grow as the drive progressed. It was all around them, like the smell of the air before a spring shower, or the tangy aroma of wood smoke on a crisp, fall day.

But it wasn't fall or spring. It was summer, and throughout the long, hot day the sun had beat relentlessly down on the men and animals below. Mercifully, the yellow glare of the early summer sky mellowed into the steel blue of late afternoon by the time the herd reached the place where it would be halted for the night, and the two men were refreshed with a breath of cool air. To the west, the sun dropped all the way to the foothills, while in the east the evening purple, like bunches of violets, gathered in the notches and timbered draws. Behind the setting sun, great bands of color spread out along the horizon. Those few clouds that dared to intrude on this perfect day were underlit by the sun, and they glowed orange in the darkening sky.

John was watching the sunset with appreciation for its beauty when he heard Linus call to him.

"I'm over here, Linus," John called back.

Linus rode over to John, and the two of them looked toward the colorful display for a few quiet moments.

"I've heard tell that the sunsets at sea are near 'bout as pretty as the ones we have out here," Linus said quietly, almost reverently. "But iffen you ask me, God'd be hard-pressed to make any sunsets better'n this here'n we're alookin' at."

"We're doin' the right thing, ain't we, Linus? Drivin' the herd up to Kansas by ourselves?"

"You havin' second thoughts?"

"Not really, I guess. Still, iffen the Indians was to try an' take the herd, there wouldn't be nothin' we could do to stop 'em."

"Look, we talked this out before we left Texas. We could'a put our hunnert beeves in with the Toothacher spread an' taken three dollars less a head at the pens. Or we could bring 'em up by ourselves, cut out a few for the Indians when they demanded their toll, an' come out a couple hunnert dollars ahead of the game up in Kansas. This is the best way."

"I guess you're right," John agreed. "Anyway, we been in Indian Territory for more'n a week now, an' we ain't had the first lick of trouble."

"An' if you ask me, we ain't gonna have no trouble," Linus said. "Whose time is it to cook supper tonight?"

"Yours."

"I'll get it started, then. How would you feel about a nice roast chicken? Maybe some mashed taters, creamed com, some greens an' corn muffins?"

"An' a cherry pie?"

"Yeah, that too."

"I don't know. I think I'd rather just have some beans," John replied, then laughed. It was a game they played to make the unvarying fare of beans or stew seem more palatable.

"All right, if beans is what you want, beans is what you get," Linus replied. He rode over to find a campsite and start supper, while John circled around the herd, singing to them, soothing them, and settling them in for the night.

Showdown at Comanche Butte

Chapter 2

"SEE IFFEN you can knock that leaner plumb offen there, Eli," Fred Geers called to his partner.

Eli spit in his hands and rubbed them together, then held the horseshoe in front of his eyes, sighting on the stake in the far pit.

"He's gonna do it," a spectator said.

"The hell he is. I'll tell you what he's gonna do. What he's gonna do is knock that there horseshoe right down onto the stake an' I'm gonna have me another ringer," Cecil Burge boasted. Cecil was one of the players from the other team. Cecil and his partner were the champion horseshoe throwers of Abesville, Missouri, and they had come to Galena to play against Fred Geers, the court barber, and Eli Byrd, the town blacksmith. Fred and Eli were champions of Galena and had been for three years running. Last year they were also champions of Stone County, and they were defending their title today.

"Come on, Eli, you can do it. The honor of Galena is at stake," one of the townspeople called. Nearly three dozen men and half as many boys had gathered around the horseshoe pit that was located under a large elm tree in the courtyard.

"Careful, Eli. Careful," someone urged.

9

Eli rocked back and forth, then swung his arm forward, tossing the shoe. It knocked Cecil's leaner away, hooked onto the top of the stake, spun around three times, then dropped with a satisfying clang as a ringer. The toss guaranteed the win and everyone cheered lustily-

"That's five dollars I won on that game. Five easy dollars," someone said happily.

"Easy for you, maybe. Fred an' Eli are the ones worked for it. What do they get out of it?"

"Hell, I'll buy 'em a drink. I'll buy ever'one a drink," the man said in a burst of generosity.

"Come on, boys, 'fore he changes his mind." Most of those who had been watching the horseshoe match started toward the Rusty Bucket to collect their free drinks.

A tall, strapping man with wide, square shoulders and a stubble-blue chin was leaning against the comer of the courthouse. Though he was not actually a part of the crowd, he had been watching the match for the last few minutes.

"Marshal Remington?"

The man turned when he heard his name. He had been called by Abner Peabody, one of the clerks for Judge Samuel Parkhurst Barnstall's Territorial Court, Stone County District.

"Yes?" Ned Remington's iron-gray eyes narrowed as he looked toward Peabody. It wasn't an act of hostility; it was just a habit of his ... a way of focusing all his attention on the subject at hand. It had been the last thing many a gunfighter had ever seen, and even though the clerk had nothing to fear from the marshal, the sight of those cold, dark slits made him uneasy.

Abner cleared his throat nervously. "Judge Barnstall would like to see you when you get a chance," he said.

"Is he in his office now?" Ned asked.

"Yes, sir."

"Then there's no time like the present," Ned replied.

Ned climbed the steps that led to Judge Barnstall's second-floor office. He tapped once on the door, then, hearing the judge's invitation, pushed it open and stepped inside.

Judge Barnstall's office was small, neat, and lined with bookshelves chock-full of law books. On one wall were two maps, one of the Southwestern United States, and the other of the Indian Nations, done on parchment. There was also a framed law degree from Harvard. Prominent in a corner was a large globe on a walnut stand, close to a mahogany liquor cabinet that displayed a crystal decanter filled with brandy and a set of snifters.

Behind the judge's desk was a leather chair, and on his desk was a stack of papers next to a wooden pen. There were two plaques on the desk, one was his name, and the other bore the legend: *Ignorantia legis neminen excusat.* A carved mahogany cigar box sat at the front. Judge Barnstall indicated the box with his hand, and Ned opened it, then pulled out a long, narrow, panatela.

Judge Barnstall looked up at Ned through piercing blue eyes. Though under six feet tall, the judge was a big man who had cast quite a shadow over the district since taking the bench.

"I heard cheering," he said. "I take it our boys won?"

"Yes," Ned said, chuckling. "I reckon it's being replayed down at the Rusty Bucket about now.

Tilghman offered to buy everyone drinks." Ned lit his cigar and a cloud of aromatic blue smoke began to drift toward the ceiling.

"Tilghman's buying drinks, is he? That would be quite a thing to see in itself. Did he get hit on the head with a horseshoe? Or was he just carried away by the exuberance of the moment?"

"I'm not sure what got into him, Judge," Ned replied with a chuckle.

"Well, I'll try to slip away from my desk in a while," Judge Barnstall went on. "Maybe I'll buy a drink for the champions of Stone County. When I do, I'll give them your best."

"You'll give them my best?"

"I'll have to. You won't be there," Barnstall said. He slid an envelope across toward Ned. "I've got a batch of warrants for you to serve. All of 'em in the Nations."

Ned picked up the envelope. "Anyone in here I know?"

"Ever heard of Tom Blue?"

"Yeah, I know 'im," Ned said. "Comanche with a cut nose, a knife scar across one cheek."

"How well do you know him?"

"I gave him the scar," Ned said matter-of-factly. "What'd he do?"

"The warrant's for stealing a couple of beef cattle from some folks who were traveling out near the buttes in western Oklahoma. I suspect he's guilty of a few other things, as well."

"I suspect he's guilty of a lot of other things," Ned said. "But, if we have a warrant for stealing a couple of cows, that's enough to get him in."

"Three others besides," Barnstall went on. "You might want to take the Black Maria so you have some way of getting them all back." The Black Maria was a jail wagon, painted black, with barred windows. "All right. I'll get Jim Early to drive it," Ned said.

"Ned, you're going pretty deep into the Nations. ... I hope you're planning on taking more than one deputy with you."

"It would probably be a good idea," Ned agreed. "All right, I'll take Dan Norling and Kurt Hammer, too."

"That's more like it," Judge Barnstall said. "When are you going to get started?"

"First light tomorrow, I reckon," Ned replied. "I'll start rounding up my deputies now."

"Early's down at the jail. You'll find Kurt in the back room, studying one of my law books," the judge said. "The only one you'll have to go after is the big Swede."

When Ned went into the back room he saw the German sitting at a narrow, square table, the book open before him, his chin resting on his hands, deep in study. His intention to become a practicing lawyer was known and respected by all the deputies who rode for Ned Remington. Kurt was square-jawed, blond-headed, and blue-eyed. He had a habit of thinking about something so deeply that he often seemed detached. This detachment gave him a sense of aloofness which many people found distracting. It didn't bother Ned.

"Find some interesting nugget of the law, my friend?" Ned asked.

"Ja," Kurt answered, looking up from his book and smiling. "Listen to this." Kurt began reading.

"'In pleading self-defense, there is a distinction between justifiable and excusable homicide.' If homicide is necessary to save a man from grievous harm it is justifiable. But, if the man was in no danger at all but was the victim of a practical joker with a pistol loaded only with blanks and he kills his assailant, the killing it not justified, but is *is* excusable."

"If some damn fool goes after another with blanks and doesn't tell him about it, he deserves to be killed," Ned said.

Kurt closed the book and pushed it to one side. "There are so many intricate things to American criminal law that I think perhaps I will never earn my degree," he said.

"Sure you will," Ned assured him. "Hell, you got the best teacher in the United States in Judge Barnstall."

"Ja, that is true," Kurt agreed. He ran his hand through his short, blond hair. "So, you have a job for me, no?"

"I have a job for you, yes," Ned said. "I have some warrants to serve in the Nations and I would like you to come along."

"Good, good," Kurt said. "I look forward to it. I was getting . . . how do you say . . . stale ... at so much study."

"We leave at first light in the morning," Ned said. "If you have any business you need to take care of, you'd better get it done now."

13

Ned walked down the back stairs to the bottom floor and the jail. There were eight cells here, but only two were occupied. The prisoners brought in by Ned's deputies didn't stay here long. They were either transferred to a federal or state prison, or they were executed.

Ned walked by the cells. One of the prisoners was lying on his bunk, his hands folded behind his head, staring morosely at the ceiling. Judge Barnstall had just sentenced him to fifteen years in prison for armed robbery, and he was waiting to be transferred. By contrast, the other prisoner, sentenced by the local magistrate, had only six days remaining on a thirty-day disturbance of the peace charge. He was a big black who worked for Eli Byrd.

"Marshal, what be the cheerin'?" the black prisoner asked as Ned walked by. "Did Mista Eli win the match?"

"That he did, Big Troy, that he did," Ned said.

"I knowed he'd do it," Big Troy said, smiling happily and slapping his fist into his hand.

"What you so excited for, nigger?" the other prisoner asked. "You ain't out there celebratin'." The prisoner had been making derisive comments and racial slurs about Big Troy for the last several days.

Ned looked over at the prisoner. "Suppose I just let him into your cell so the two of you can have a private celebration? How about that, Big Troy? Would you like to help this fellow celebrate?"

Big Troy looked over at the white prisoner and saw him grow even whiter at the prospect of being left alone with the subject of his slurs. Big Troy smiled.

"Yes, suh, I reckon I could help him real good."

"You ain't gonna do that, are you, Marshal?" The white prisoner blanched.

"I might," Ned replied, "if you don't watch your big mouth."

Ned stepped into the front office and saw Deputy Marshal James Ransom Early. Early was sitting in a chair tipped back against the wall. On the wall behind him was a spate of Wanted posters and a Currier and Ives print of two trains racing out of Washington, D.C., both of them trailing smoke and fire. Early was a lean, nearly skinny man, but with muscles as hard as dried-out leather. He was a quiet man who studied the world through iron-gray eyes. He was wearing a .44- caliber Remington revolver low on his hip. The pistol had once been a cap-and-ball, but with the substitution of a new cylinder and hammer, now accommodated brass cartridges.

Early was drinking a cup of coffee. He offered a cup to Ned, typically without speaking, but merely by making a motion with his cup.

Ned picked up a blue coffeepot, walked over and freshened Early's coffee, then poured a cup for himself. He sat the pot back on top of the little stove.

"We're taking a little trip into the Nations," Ned said.

Early just nodded.

"I want you to drive the Black Maria," Ned added, taking a swallow of his coffee.

"How many are we going after?"

"At least four," Ned said. "Maybe more before it's all done. I'm taking the Swede and the German with us."

"Good men to have along," Early agreed. "When are we leaving?"

"Tomorrow morning, first light. "I've told Kurt already. I've got to ride out to tell Norling."

"You'll be seeing Katy?"

"Yes."

"Give her my best," Early said.

"Thanks, Jim, she'll appreciate that," Ned replied.

Ned finished his coffee, then left through the front door. It was a ride of several minutes out to the convent to see Katy. It was a ritual he went through before every trip out . . . this seeing his daughter to tell her good-bye, to reassure her that he loved her. She needed his reassurance and his love if she was ever going to recover from the sickness that had come over her after seeing her mother raped and murdered, then herself being raped and left for dead.

The doctors told Ned that there were some things medicine didn't yet understand, and one of them was what happened to a person's mind when they were subjected to such horror as had befallen Katy. She was a grown woman . . . but she couldn't, or wouldn't, talk. There was nothing wrong with her physically, but she was as crippled as if she had been paralyzed.

When the doctors said there was nothing more they could do for her, Ned took her to a convent. There she was looked after, prayed for, and loved. Ned visited her as often as he could, always talking to her, telling her amusing or exciting stories, assuring her of his love. For a long time he had no idea whether she even heard him or not. Then one day she looked at him and said, ". . . love you." She had advanced very little beyond those two words . . . but she had advanced, and Ned still hoped and prayed for the miracle of full recovery. He knew that someday it would happen.

Chapter 3

NED TIED HIS HORSE to the hitching rail in front of the Morning Star Hotel in Crane, Missouri. A large banner stretched from one side of the porch to the other, proclaiming Crane's "Third Annual Quilting Bee and Social Gathering." Just inside, in the hotel lobby, there were more than a dozen quilts on display, each showing the colorful patterns and intricate needlework of the quilters' art.

To the right of the lobby was a door leading back to the dining room. Though many people were looking at the quilts, they were drawn toward the dining room by the delicious aromas that drifted enticingly through the door.

Ned nodded at a few of the people who were in the lobby. He walked through the dining room where white-jacketed waiters were busily setting up the tables for the gala dinner, then into the kitchen, to an atmosphere of steaming caldrons and banging pans, rattling pots and sizzling meats. There were half a dozen cooks, all talking at once, but in the center of all the excitement, directing the activity of the others, stood a tall, powerfully built man. He was very much in charge, and he wore his apron and cook's hat with as much authority as a general wears his uniform.

"Hello, Dan," Ned said to the tall cook.

Dan, who was holding a meat cleaver in his hand, looked over at Ned. He saw that Ned was wearing denim trousers, a red flannel shirt, and a leather vest. His Colt was strapped low on his hip. The marshal was obviously not here for the dinner.

"We have business, I see," Dan said.

"Yes."

"All right, I come now."

Dan started to put down the cleaver, but Ned held his hand out toward him.

"No need to stop what you're doin'," he said. "We won't leave 'til first light in the mornin'. I'd hate to be the cause of these nice people not gettin' the meal they came for."

Dan was not an employee of the hotel, but he was known all over Stone County for his culinary skills. As a result of his fame, he was often prevailed upon to cook for special occasions. Sometimes Dan agreed, sometimes he didn't. Though he could write his own ticket as a cook just about anywhere, he refused to follow it as an avocation.

"I love cooking," he often said. "And what I love most about it is that I don't have to do it."

"You," Dan said to one of his assistants. "Fix a plate for the marshal." .

A moment later one of the kitchen workers set a plate in front of Ned.

"What is this?" Ned asked. "It looks pretty fair to middlin'."

"French veal, I call it," Dan explained. "It's veal coated in egg and breadcrumbs, stuffed with ham and cheese, and browned in butter."

"Uhmm, look at that," Ned said.

"Look at it good, Marshal," an ominous voice hissed, " 'cause they ain't gonna have nothin' like that in hell." The words were followed by the unmistakable metallic click of a hammer locking into the sear of a revolver.

Ned turned toward the sound of the voice and saw a small, bandy-legged man with a scraggly black beard and beady brown eyes, holding a gun on him. He didn't look as if the gun were an unfamiliar tool for him. One of the cooks started toward the intruder.

"Gary, stay away from him," Dan warned.

"That's good advice, Gary," the man with the gun said menacingly.

"Who are you?" Gary demanded, paying no attention to Dan or the gunman. "What are you doing in my kitchen? You have no right—"

Gary's complaint was suddenly cut short by the roar of a pistol shot. The cook's face contorted in an expression of surprise. He grabbed his chest as if trying to hold his life in with his bare hands. Blood spilled through his fingers, then he fell against the wall and slid down to the floor, leaving a wide smear of red on the wall behind him. He died in the sitting position.

"Anybody else doesn't want to listen to good advice?" the gunman asked.

"What's going on back here? What's the shooting?" someone yelled, running into the kitchen from the dining room.

"You, big man," the gunman said to Dan. "This fella didn't listen to you. You better make the others listen or there'll be someone else dead besides Gary here, an' the marshal, who's fixin' to join him."

"Stay back," Dan called, waving them back with his cleaver. "All of you, stay out of here." The head waiter, who was the first man through the door, saw the dead cook on the floor, then quickly heeded Dan's advice.

"You're planning to kill me?" Ned asked.

"That's right."

"Who are you?"

"The name's Brubaker. That mean anythin' to you?"

"Harlan Brubaker? Yes, I have a warrant to serve you," Ned replied. "I was just getting ready to come after you in the morning."

Brubaker laughed. "Now, ain't that somethin'? You got a warrant to serve. Well I'm savin' you the trip. You don't have to come after me, 'cause I'm already here. Say your prayers, Marshal."

Brubaker raised his pistol level with Ned's head and cocked it a second time. Everyone in the kitchen tensed as they waited for the explosion of the shot. Suddenly there was a whistling sound, then a solid thunk. Brubaker let out a gasp and dropped his pistol and staggered toward the wall. A meat cleaver jutted from the junction of his neck and shoulder. Dan Norling's eyes glittered with a silent satisfaction. Brubaker made a feeble, clawing effort to pull the cleaver out, then fell, face down, across the legs of the man he had just shot. He gasped one more time then was quiet.

"Well," Ned said. "I guess we can scratch one name off our list."

Norling grinned obscenely.

The sun wasn't yet visible, but the eastern sky was streaked with bands of pink and gray as the men moved out of Galena the next morning. The streets were empty and the hollow clump of the horses' hooves sounded exceptionally loud in the quietness of morning. Jim Early sat on the driver's seat of the Black Maria, holding the ribbons loosely in his hands. The wheels rolled easily, well greased for the trip. A dog ran out and nipped at the wheels a couple of times, but he didn't bark.

Ned looked at the men he was taking with him. As Dan had proved last night, and all had proved on more than one occasion, they were good men to have around. Actually every man who made up the special force of deputies for Judge Barnstall's court was exceptional.

Jim Early, his driver, was probably second-in-charge of the group. He was a quiet, hard-bitten man with a strong sense of right and wrong. Ned tried not to make close friends ... in this business that wasn't a very productive thing to do. But if he had to pick the man he was closest to, it would probably be Jim Early. Jim knew all about Katy . . . was the only one of the deputies, who visited her regularly. Jim had drunk a drink with Ned in quiet celebration when Katy said her first words. When Ned had given Jim's regards to Katy last night, he was sure he saw a look of recognition in her eyes, though she didn't say anything. Still, his visit with her wasn't as depressing as they once were. He knew now that she did hear him when he talked to her, did know when he kissed her good-bye.

From Jim, driving the wagon, Ned turned his attention to the two men who were riding alongside him.

Kurt Hammer was a German, an immigrant who left Germany after learning that a degree from the University of Heidelberg didn't mean much if you didn't have the right connections. Especially if you killed the wrong man in a duel. Though it was clearly self defense, Kurt had barely managed to beat the police out of the country. He was the best educated of all the deputies and was studying law. One day soon Kurt would hang up his pistols and take up a book of Mr. Blackstone. Ned wasn't looking forward to that day . . . Kurt was a hard-working, dependable man and good to have around in a pinch. But Ned would be glad for him when he reached his goal.

Dan Norling was the best traveled and most adventurous of all the deputies. He had sailed around the world three times as a ship's bosun, worked in Hong Kong as a warehouseman and, according to rumor, was once a cook for the Bey of Istanbul. He so impressed that august gentleman that Dan was offered a fortune in gold and jewels, the only requirement being that he allow himself to be castrated so he could serve in the bey's personal household. Dan left Istanbul quickly, on the same day as the offer.

Ned had never asked Dan if the story was true, and had no desire to. All he knew was that as good as Dan Norling was with a meat cleaver, he was twice as good with a six-gun in his hand. Unfortunately, though, Dan's skills in a kitchen, where he was adequately supplied with all the utensils and equipment necessary to turn out gourmet meals, did not extend to his trail cooking. Ned's first big disappointment was in learning that Dan Norling's trail beans and beef tasted just like everybody else's trail beans and beef.

Three days after Ned and his deputies left Galena, and about ten miles farther west than they had reached, John Duncan was slowly circling his one hundred head of beeves. The pre-dawn morning was dark except for distant heat lightning flickering along the horizon, momentarily lighting the herd and the empty stretches of the Oklahoma prairie.

John and his partner, Linus Rawlings, had been in Indian Territory for three weeks now, and it was beginning to look as if their pre-trail fears had been unfounded.

John crooned a soft lullaby to the cows. Despite the heat lightning, the animals were quiet. They had been a good herd, trailing easily from the Red River up to the Washita, the Canadian, and the Cimarron. Since coming through Indian Territory there had been good grass and water, and they lost only three beeves, given to the Indians as toll. They had prepared for that; in fact, they could give up seven more and still get into Kansas with a hundred head.

John came around the herd to the spot where Linus had thrown out his bedroll. Linus had watched the herd until midnight, John from midnight till dawn. It would be first light by the time John circled the herd again so it was time to wake Linus, have him start the coffee and a little breakfast. He saw movement in the camp.

"Ho, so you're up already, Linus," he called. "Well, it'll save me the trouble of—" Suddenly John tensed. It wasn't anything he could put his finger on. ... He hadn't heard anything, or seen anything other than the moving shadow he had spied when he first rode up. Still, there was something not quite right here. "Linus?" he called.

Heat lightning flashed again, disclosing a short but powerfully built man, long black hair, obsidian eyes, a badly cut nose and a long scar running across a red cheek. The man was an Indian, and he held a knife in front of him. The knife blade was smeared red with blood.

"What the hell?" John called. His horse, frightened by the shout, bolted forward. As it turned out, it was a fortunate move for the rider, because there was more than one Indian in the camp and one of them fired. Had John's horse not bolted at just that moment, he might have been hit by the bullet he heard whizzing by.

John wasn't carrying his gun. His pistol and rifle were back in the camp, lying on top of his bedroll. They generally carried weapons by day but left them off at night, figuring that a sudden shot might spook the herd and send them into a stampede. The wisdom of their argument was proved now as the cattle started running with the sound of the Indian's shot.

John bent low over his horse and urged the animal toward the stampeding cows. The beeves were running without a sound other than that made by their hooves. As they ran, heat welled up in their bodies and beat against John's face.

Under normal circumstances John would be trying to stop the herd, but now he urged them on. The Indians were right behind him and he wanted to put the cattle between him and them.

John managed to circle the herd, then he dashed away from them, letting them run pell-mell across the plain. He traveled half a mile in a little over a minute, while the sounds grew more muffled behind him. When he twisted in his saddle he saw that the Indians had given up on him and were in full pursuit of his herd. He was safe.

John rode into a draw and hid there until it was full light. He watched the prairie for a long time before he abandoned the security of his hiding place. Finally, when he was convinced that the Indians were gone, he mounted his horse and started riding. He went first to the camp to see about Linus.

He thought he was going to be sick. Linus had more than a dozen arrows sticking out of his body, and the scalp had been removed from his head. His stomach had been cut open and there were long gashes in his thighs and arms. John leaned against the side of his horse for a moment, fighting the nausea and dizziness. Linus was more than his friend and partner. He was married to his wife's sister. He didn't look forward to going back home with this news.

John looked around the camp and saw that everything they had was gone. The guns, the packhorse with the food and cooking utensils, even the blankets and tarps they had used for the bedrolls. He realized now that he was stranded, hundreds of miles from nowhere, with no food and no weapons. He had escaped the Indians, but he wasn't yet out of danger.

There was no shovel, but John managed to dig a hole with the branch of a tree. He dropped Linus's body into the hole without so much as a blanket, then covered it up with rocks and dirt. He looked around to fix the place in his mind.

If he never came back, he could at least describe the burying ground to the widow.

Chapter 4

NED AND HIS DEPUTIES ran into John Duncan at midmorning. Duncan had been pushing his horse pretty hard, and the animal was showing the results of his efforts, blowing hard and foamed with yellowish ropes of sweat.

"Mister," Early said. "Bein' as that's your horse, I guess I got no business buttin' in like this. But you're gonna kill 'im if you ride 'im another hour like that."

"I know, I know," the rider said nervously, himself nearly as winded as his mount. He patted the horse on the neck. "He's a good horse, he deserves better'n the way I'm treatin' him." He looked at the four men, saw the badges on their vests, the bars on the wagon. "Who are you?" he asked.

"I'm Ned Remington, United States Marshal," Ned said. "These are my deputies, Early, Norling, and Hammer. Who are you?"

"John Duncan."

"You live here in the Nations, do you, Duncan?"

"No. Me an' my partner got a small spread just over the line down in Texas."

"What are you doing up here in Indian Territory?"

"We're takin' the Chisholm Trail," John started, then he stopped. "That is, we was takin' the trail. We was movin' our

25

cattle up to the railhead in Kansas. But we was jumped this mornin' before we broke camp. My partner was kilt and our cows was stole, along with ever'thin' else we had . . . guns, camp gear, packhorse. I was lucky to get out alive. Reckon the reason I run my horse like I done was I was pure scairt to death."

"Who hit you?"

"Indians," Duncan said. He ran his hand through his hair. "I thought the Indians up here was civilized. I thought they had towns an' schools just like white folk."

"You're talking of the eastern tribes," Ned said. "The ones the government moved here from back east. If you were on the Chisholm Trail you ran into the western Indians . . . Kiowa, perhaps, or Comanche."

"I guess so. Anyway, I thought Indians didn't make war in the dark. It wasn't even light yet when they hit us."

"Doesn't sound to me like it was much of a war," Ned said. "You say there was just the two of you?"

"Yeah."

"Then it wasn't a real war party, just a bunch of renegades."

"I guess so. You know, we been in the territory for two weeks. We've seen a few Indians but most of 'em just left us alone. A couple or three times we cut out a head or two to give 'em, an' they went on their way. These here Indians didn't even palaver none. They just come up an' took over."

"Indians, even from the western tribes, are pretty much like everybody else," Ned said. "You got those that behave themselves, and you got those who go bad and raise a little ruckus."

"A little ruckus? They kilt my partner, stole my herd. In my book that ain't no little ruckus, that's a major rampage."

"I guess you could call it that," Ned agreed. "By the way, did you get a look at any of them?"

"You kiddin'? All I wanted was to get the hell outta there. I wasn't goin' to stay aroun' an' see what they look like. The one I saw was ugly enough, what with that cut nose an' scar across his cheek."

"You sure about that?" Ned asked. "He had a cut nose and a scar here?"-Ned made a motion with his hand across his own face.

"Yeah," Duncan said. "Yeah, that's him."

"That's Tom Blue, all right," Early said.

"What? You mean you know this redskin?" Duncan asked.

"We know him," Ned said. "I've got a warrant for his arrest right now. He stole a couple of cows from a fella last month."

"A couple of cows? That's all you got on him? You ain't goin' after him for a couple of cows, I hope. I'll swear out a warrant against the heathen sonofabitch for murder."

"Don't need it," Ned said.

"What do you mean, you don't need it?" Duncan asked in surprise. "You mean you ain't even gonna let me take out a warrant on the sonofabitch?"

Ned looked at Kurt. "What about it, Kurt? You're the lawyer here. Do I need another warrant?"

"No," Kurt answered. "A warrant served for one crime may be upgraded after the prisoner is in custody if there is evidence that another crime was committed before the arrest was made."

"It just don't seem right that you ain't gonna arrest him for killin' Linus," Duncan said.

"Look at it this way, Duncan. If we go back to Galena to get that warrant, Blue will have another week's head start on us. The warrant we have will arrest him just as easy," Early said.

"Maybe easier," Ned suggested. "If he thinks that's all we got on him, he may come in without a straggle."

"All right," Duncan agreed. "I ... I suppose it makes no difference as long as he's arrested."

"You can come along with us if you want . . . point him out," Ned said.

27

"I . . .I thought you said you knew him."

"I do."

"Then, if it's all the same to you, I'd just as soon get on back down to Texas," Duncan said. "I gotta tell Linus' widow. And 'twixt you an' me . . .I don't ever want to look at that Indian's ugly face again. I reckon you can call me a coward if you want."

"Not coward," Norling said, speaking for the first time. "Just good sense, I'd say."

"I hope you get him," Duncan said as he turned south. "All I can say is, I hope you get him."

"Oh, we'll get him, Mr. Duncan," Ned said matter-of-factly. "That's what we're getting paid for."

"Good. I'll sleep better knowin' that heathens like that are bein' dealt with. Good luck to you fellas." Early snapped the reins and the team started forward, the three men riding alongside.

"So," Ned said, "Tom Blue isn't content to steal a couple of cows. Now he takes the whole herd."

"*Ja.* And kills someone besides," Kurt added. "Him, I will be glad to catch," Dan said.

It rained the next day, a rain that slanted almost horizontally out of the northeast, driven by a wind that made a sustained roar around them. Overhead, black clouds scudded darkly along, sometimes obscuring the tops of the low hills through which the men rode.

All four men were wearing slickers that flapped noisily in the wind, hats that dripped water in cascades whenever they moved their heads. The hooves of the horses and the wheels of the wagon slipped and slid on the slick, wet ground beneath. The rain kept up until early afternoon when it settled into a steady drizzling, without much wind. Horses and wagon plodded along, into sagebrush and grass and rolling plain. It was near supper time when they spotted the settlement ahead.

Sand Springs wasn't much, a single street formed by a road that wandered in off the prairie and, after a few hundred yards or so, wandered out again. There were no more than ten buildings in the entire town.

There was a livery bam separated from a hotel by a vacant lot. Next to the hotel was a cafe, and next to that a mercantile store. Across the street stood a one- room log building, sod-roofed and probably chinked with the original mud mixed when it was finished. Alongside the soddy was a house built of whipsawed, unpainted lumber.

Sand Springs was said to be the home territory of Red Hailey. Red had robbed a bank up in Kansas, and his name was on one of the warrants Ned was carrying.

The little group of lawmen halted in front of the cafe, then swung stiffly to the ground. They looped the horses' reins around the rail and waded through the mud to the boardwalk, where they stopped long enough to stamp part of the mud from their boots. Then they removed their hats and batted them against their legs. A shower of rain water sprayed from them, then the men put the soggy, misshapen hats back on again.

The cafe was no more impressive than the town itself. Half a dozen homemade tables, a counter with whipsawed two-inch planks, and a squat iron heating stove—cold now, but desperately needed in the winter—made up all the furnishings. There was a jar of pickled boiled eggs on the counter.

Ned caught the smell of whiskey, though the sale of whiskey in this part of Oklahoma was strictly forbidden. Someone came down to them.

"Can I help you gents?" he asked. "An' don't ask for nothin' to drink. That's ag'in the law and this here is a law-abidin' place."

"How law abiding would you be if you hadn't seen our badges or the jail wagon we have parked out front?" Ned asked.

"Be the same," the man said without changing expression. "You want somethin' to eat?"

"Anything but beans."

"Got some pork chops, fried potatoes," the man offered.

"Sounds good," Ned agreed.

Forty-five minutes later the men pushed empty plates away, satisfied by a meal that wasn't trail-cooked. Jim left to take care of the horses, Dan and Kurt went out to take a look around the town. Ned decided to stay and have another cup of coffee. He picked the cup up, carried it halfway to his mouth, when he heard his name.

"You Remington? Are you Ned Remington?"

Ned's hand stopped, the cup still several inches away from his mouth. There was the sound of challenge in that voice, and he knew he was about to be pushed into a showdown.

"That's me," he said. •

"Marshal Ned Remington," the voice said, coming down hard on the word *marshal,* saying it in a taunting tone.

Ned looked toward the speaker and saw a young man in his early twenties. He was wearing a hat, but Ned could see enough of his hair to notice that it was red.

"You must be Red Hailey."

"Come after me, did you?" Red asked. There was a recklessness in the young man's demeanor, but a nervous flickering of fear in his eyes. More than recklessness or fear, though, was the glint of excitement, crackling like lightning in the young man's glance. Red Hailey was clearly a man who was prepared to put his entire life on the line just for the pure thrill of it.

"Maybe," Ned said.

Red's right hand moved over the butt of his pistol. His fingers opened and closed nervously.

"You're gonna have to kill me to take me in," he said.

"Red, far as I know, the only paper we got against you is for stealing," Ned said calmly. "That hardly seems worth getting killed for, or killing for."

"That don't matter none. If you've come after me, you're gonna have to go up against me. Let's see how fast you are, Marshal."

"You don't have to do this, son."

Red's face hardened, his eyes narrowed. "Don't call me son," he said.

Ned sighed, then stood up and faced the young man. "All right, Red, let's do it," he said.

Ned looked into Red's eyes. He would see it there first ... the moment the young man decided to make his play. The eyes showed fear, excitement, then, at the last second, indecision. Had he made a mistake? Should he have pushed it this far? Too late; he couldn't back out now. The eyes showed resignation, and that's when Ned knew he would start his move.

Red made a frantic, clawing grab for his gun. Ned's own hand moved instantly and automatically. He felt the grip of the .44's butt against his palm, felt the weight of the pistol as he snicked it from his holster. He thumbed the hammer back, then ticked the trigger with his finger. The gun fired and bucked in his hand. His nose wrinkled as the acrid smell of exploded black powder burned his nostrils.

Red let out a grunting sound as the heavy .44 slug caught him in the chest. His expression twisted into a mask of complete surprise. He had not thought it would end like this. He fell heavy on his back, his hands thrown out to each side, the pistol, still unfired, clattering to the floor beside him.

Ned looked at the others in the cafe.

"I'm a United States Marshal," he said. "I have a warrant for this man's arrest. I would have preferred to serve it, but you saw what happened. I would appreciate it if one of you would draw up a paper telling what you saw, and the rest of you would sign it."

"I'll do it, Marshal," someone said.

The door opened then, and Ned's three deputies came in. They took one look at the man on the floor, then knew what happened without having to be told.

"He on our list?" Jim asked.

"Red Hailey," Ned said. "He robbed a bank up in Kansas."

The town sheriff came in then, saw the body, then saw Ned and the deputies. He knew them.

31

"I wondered when the boy would get too big for his britches," the sheriff said. He nodded at a couple of men. "Get 'im out of here, down to Donaldson's. Tell Ed to pick out a pine box; the town'll pay for it."

Two of the customers picked up the body and carried him out, one under the head, the other at the feet.

"I had a warrant for him, but I never got to serve it," Ned said.

"Got a warrant for anyone else from my town?" the sheriff asked.

"Don't think so. Got one for Tom Blue for cattle stealing, another for Nate Luckless for selling whiskey to the Indians."

"Cattle stealing all you got on Tom Blue?" the sheriff wanted to know.

"It's the only warrant we have," Ned said. "We believe he killed a cattleman a few days ago."

"A cattleman? Hell, he and his band of cutthroats killed a whole family last week."

"Where?"

"You haven't heard? The Doomey ranch, about a hundred miles west of here. Their neighbors found them. Doomey and his two hands were dead and scalped, the woman and two little girls was in the kitchen, shot."

"Chris Doomey?" Kurt asked.

"You know him?" Ned wanted to know.

"I know him," Kurt said. "He's my cousin."

"How do you know Tom Blue did it?" Ned asked the sheriff.

"Hell, who else could it be? There's only one bunch of renegade redskins running loose in the Nations." Ned sighed. "You're right. Who else could it be?"

Chapter 5

SIXTEEN-YEAR-OLD Laurel Hope sat on the seat, warm and lazy, dozing as the wagon moved along ever so slowly across the gentle rolling plains. As the steel- rimmed wheels creaked over the sun-baked earth, they kicked up dirt, causing a rooster tail of dust to stream out behind them. The wood of the wagons was bleached white, and under the sun it gave off a warm, pleasant smell. Laurel concentrated on the unlit, dangling lantern at the rear of the wagon in front of them. Laurel, her father Emil, her mother Lucinda, and her little sister Penny had joined their wagon with eleven other wagons. Thirty-five men, women and children were part of a wagon train that had come down from Kansas. They had been on the trail for eight weeks through country cut up by ravines and brooks, and choked draws rampant with entangling thickets. Now they emerged upon a great prairie, an expanse of rumpled short-grass plains with occasional clumps of trees dimly seen in the distance, like tiny islands in a sea. This was the western border of a scattered belt of forest land, about forty miles in width, which stretched across the country from north to south, from the Arkansas to the Red River. This oddly fashioned landscape was called the Cross Timbers.

Laurel looked around with interest at this open country she would soon call home. Though it often got unbearably hot during the day, Laurel liked the summer, full as it was with wild flowers growing in colorful profusion amid the verdant grasses. Laurel had kept a record of every flower she could identify and so far had listed gaillardias, burgundy cups, poppy mallows, the blue and white lupinelike drapes of loco- weed, pink and blue grass starflowers, sunflowers, milkweed, the white flames of yucca candles, and the drooping green-white blossoms of chinaberries. Redbuds and white haws followed the streams, and in the open country the wild sand plums perfumed the air with their fragrance. Over it all arched a sky of incredible turquoise blue, sometimes splotched with white thunderheads, other times blackened with low, elephantine clouds that signaled the oncoming storms. At night Laurel felt she could reach up and pull down stars from the blue-black velvet cloak of the sky.

It had been an easy, peaceful trip. Water was plentiful, there was grass for grazing, and almost every day men of the train brought in game to eat. Even the Indians had been friendly. Whenever they encountered them—and they generally ran across a party about every week or so—there was a prescribed ritual they went through. Actually, her father said, it was a form of controlled blackmail. The Indians would arrive, generally in war paint, make a few motions, such as riding their horses toward the wagons and brandishing bows and arrows or war lances, then turn away at the last minute. A couple of the men from the wagon train would then ride out to meet them, offer some token of friendship, and the Indians would allow them to pass in peace. Laurel even began to look forward to the appearance of the Indians, for it always broke up the monotony of the travel.

Tom Blue sat with the others around the council fire and studied the faces of the elders and warriors. Their faces and chests were bathed orange by the wavering flames of the council fire, while behind there was only the blue-blackness of night. Tiny, glowing sparks rode the smoke up into the night sky, scattering red stars among the brittle pinpoints of silver. Tom Blue was here because he was the subject of discussion.

"I say that Tom Blue and those who follow him should be sent away," the speaker said. His name was Joe Pipestem, and he had once been the fastest runner in the tribe though he had married and was too fond of his woman's cooking to run anymore. "He is causing much trouble."

"You say this because you wish to stay in the village with the women. You grow fat and lazy while I fight the white men who take our land, run away our buffalo."

"You say you are fighting the white men because they take our land but that isn't true. You fight the white men so you can steal what he has and trade it for whiskey."

"I take the whiskey because white man's law says the Indian cannot have whiskey. I spit on the white man's law."

"If you stay, the soldiers will come to our village."

"Does Joe Pipestem fear the soldiers?" Tom Blue taunted.

"If war comes with honor, I do not fear to-fight," Joe Pipestem said. "But you have not fought with honor. There was no honor in killing a woman and two children."

"They killed themselves," Billy Blackhat said in Tom Blue's defense.

"Is the woman dead? Yes," Joe Pipestem said. "Does it matter to the soldiers whether she killed herself or you killed her? No. She is dead and the soldiers will come."

"Maybe if Tom Blue would go to the soldiers and tell them that he did this thing, that we did not do it, they would not harm us," another suggested.

"Yes," another put in quickly. "Tom Blue, would you do this thing? Would you tell the soldiers that the people of this village want only peace? That the people of this village have not harmed the white men?"

Tom Blue let out a snort of disgust, then stood up to face the council.

"Where are the brave young men?" he asked. "They are not in this council. Where are the Comanche of our forefathers, those who were feared by all their enemies? They are not in this council. When I look at the faces of those in this place of bad hearts I see the faces of women."

Tom Blue sat back down, and Joe Pipestem continued his indictment. "I have thought on this matter, Tom Blue, and now I say this: you may stay in the village for one more night only. Tomorrow, you must leave. If you come back, we will give you to the soldiers."

Tom Blue stood up again and looked at the others.

"Does Joe Pipestem speak for all of you?"

Some looked at him in defiance, some looked down, but no one answered him. Angrily, he turned and walked away from the council fire.

Tom Blue thought about the action of the council that night. He was angry with them. He wanted to show them that he was a leader who should be respected and followed, and he believed he had a way of doing just that.

Tom Blue knew that a wagon train was passing close by. He had heard some of the others talking about extorting gifts from them. He had spat in disgust when he heard them tell the stories. They were women, to speak of gifts. Warriors didn't have gifts bestowed upon them; warriors took what they wanted. Tom Blue decided to get some warriors to go with him.

If a white man had seen Tom Blue making preparations for the attack on the wagon train, he wouldn't have understood one thing that was going on. The white men had a compulsion for making chiefs of the Indians; war chiefs, council chiefs, high chiefs and sub-chiefs. Some white men joked that all Indians were chiefs, and though they didn't realize it, they were much closer to the truth than they imagined. The Comanche had no elected chiefs, nor did a chief obtain his position by right of inheritance. The only criterion for being a chief was leadership. If one could get others to follow, he was a chief. If they would not follow, he was not a chief, and it was that simple. Tom Blue, by persuasion, promises, deals, and threats, was able to convince ten others to follow him in his planned attack on the wagon train, and therefore he was, by every definition of the term, a war chief.

Tom Blue awoke the next morning while the position of the stars indicated there were still three hours of darkness left. He went to those who had agreed to go with him, waking them with gentle nudges, cautioning them to be quiet, then moving on to the next until all were mounted in the center circle of the village. Tom Blue held up his rifle, then let out a shout of pride and defiance as he urged them to follow.

Now the whole village was awakened, and they came to the doors of their homes and looked out at Tom Blue, who was holding a rifle over his head. Tom Blue smiled proudly, and he felt a stirring of power as he called out.

"Come, if you are brave, and join me. Join me if you are a warrior. ... Stay behind with Joe Pipestem if you are a woman or a coward!"

Though Tom Blue's defiant call challenged others by calling them a woman or coward if they stayed behind, most remembered the council meeting of the night before. They knew that Tom Blue was not a true warrior but a renegade who stood condemned by his own people. Without giving him another thought, they returned to bed as Tom Blue led his handful of men away into the darkness.

Ned led his little group of men out of Sand Springs, still heading west. Though he had originally been given warrants for four men, two of the documents were no longer valid. One man lay dead back in Missouri, the second was stretched out in a pine box in Sand Springs. Only the warrants for Tom Blue and Nate Luckless were still in effect.

"What do you know about this fella, Nate Luckless?" Jim asked. Jim was driving the Black Maria, but Ned was riding close enough alongside that they could carry on a conversation.

"I've never seen him," Ned answered. "All I know is he's been selling whiskey to the Indians, and the judge wants him out of here."

"Think he's hooked up with Tom Blue in any way?"

"I wouldn't be surprised," Ned said.

"If he is, he's guilty of a hell of a lot more than just sellin' whiskey to the Indians."

"Like with Tom Blue, though, the warrant we have is good enough to get him back to Missouri. And once we get him back there, he belongs to the judge."

"Yeah, and I wouldn't want to be in his shoes when he goes before Judge Barnstall. Especially if he had anything to do with all the killin' Tom Blue has been doin'."

Suddenly there was a loud, popping sound, and the wagon lurched hard to the right.

"Damn!" Jim swore, reining the team to a halt. "We busted a spoke."

Jim climbed down from the wagon seat while Ned, Kurt, and Dan dismounted. The right front wheel was twisted to a crazy angle and broken. Jagged pieces of a spoke were sticking out.

"Have we got a spare wheel?"

"No," Jim said. He walked around to the back of the wagon and opened the gate, unlocked now that there were no prisoners inside. "But I do have some spare spokes," he said, smiling. "All we have to do is get that wheel off, pull the busted spoke and put a new one in."

"Right," Ned said. "But first we have to get the wheel off. We better look around for a rock to set the axle on."

Tom Blue gave the reins of his pony to Rufus Coyote, then climbed to the top of a little hill. He lay behind the crest of the hill so he couldn't be seen against the skyline, then sneaked up to the top and peered over. There, below him, he saw the wagon train. It was obvious that the whites had no idea they were in danger. The fools ... they thought they could bargain their way out by giving up a hatchet, a bolt of cloth or, on rare occasions, a rifle or a horse. Let the others of his kind do that. He wasn't going to pose or prance for the white men. If they had something he wanted, he would take it.

Tom Blue smiled, then slithered back down the hill into the ravine where the others waited.

"Are the wagons there?" Rufus Coyote asked.

"Yes."

"How many on horses?"

"I see only one man on a horse. The others are driving the wagons."

Rufus Coyote smiled broadly. If there had been several men on horseback, they could have ridden out to engage the Indians during the attack, allowing the wagons time to go free. If only one man was mounted, there would be no danger of that. And the wagons were so slow and cumbersome that escape was impossible.

"It will be a good fight," Rufus Coyote said.

Tom Blue climbed onto the back of his pony, then looked at Rufus Coyote, Billy Blackhat, and the other warriors who had come with him. There were only ten now, but when word spread of his victories, when the white eyes cringed at the sound of his name, there would be more . . . many more. He felt the eyes of his followers on him, and he knew they were looking to him for leadership.

He had already proved himself. With only five men, he had killed all the whites at the Doomey ranch. With the same five men, he had taken the herd of the two white men . . . and his followers had dipped their fingers in the blood of the man he killed. Now he would lead these men in an attack against the wagon train. There were many more men on the train than he was leading, but he knew they would not be expecting an attack. Though the numbers were on the side of the whites, the advantage was all his. He held his rifle over his head and, using it, signaled the others to follow him.

It was a good day to die. It was an even better day to kill.

Chapter 6

"ARE YOU GOING to take a nap down there, Jim, or do you plan to get finished sometime today?" Ned asked. His voice was strained because he, Dan, and Kurt were holding up the comer of the Black Maria. They were waiting for Jim to slide a rock under the axle so they could let the wagon down onto it and still have the front wheel elevated. Because of the steel bars and the steel-reinforced top and bottom of the van, it was much heavier than an ordinary wagon of commerce. Holding it up was putting a hell of a strain on them.

Working in close confines beneath the wagon, Jim was having some difficulty with the rock. He was in some danger at this point, because if the three men lost their grip the wagon would fall on him.

"I'll get it," he said.

"Today?" Kurt taunted.

Jim pushed and rolled the stone, finally getting it into place. "There," he said with a grunt. "I think I've got it now."

"Slide out from under there," Ned called to him.

Jim rolled over, then scurried out from under as, with a mighty sigh of relief, the three men set the wagon down on the rock.

"I'm glad that part is over," Ned said.

"Ja," Kurt agreed. He looked at his hands. "I will be picking . . . how do you say little pieces of wood?"

"Splinters," Ned suggested.

"Ja, splinters. For one month I will pick them from my hands." .

Early started pulling the wheel. "Might as well get at it," he said.

"Do you think—" Kurt started to ask, but Ned held up a hand to stop him.

"Listen," Ned said.

"What is it?" Dan asked, puzzled by Ned's comment. "I don't hear nothing."

"Listen," Ned said again.

All four were quiet for a moment, with only the sound of the ever-present prairie wind moaning its mournful wail. Then Ned heard it again. The sound was so faint that it could barely be heard until a momentary shift in the wind carried it to their ears, and all heard it.

Thump, thump, thump.

"Gunfire," Early said, but he didn't have to say a word. There wasn't a one of them who hadn't recognized the sound.

Three of the wagons were in flames, and as they rolled pell-mell across the plains, pulled by fear-crazed horses, the men, women, and children leaped down from them and ran in terror. Tom Blue had led his little band of renegades against the train, seemingly from nowhere. The Indians had whooped and shouted as they galloped their horses right through the line of wagons. The wagon train had not broken formation, nor had they formed into a circle. The settlers had not been particularly frightened by Tom Blue's terrible charge. After all, they had already seen a dozen such "attacks," only to have the Indians break off and begin their negotiations. This time, however, it hadn't happened that way. Before anyone knew what was going on, the wagon train had come under assault, a real attack, with barking rifles and flying arrows. Fire arrows and flaming torches had already ignited three of the wagons, including the Hope wagon.

The settlers were inadequately armed. A few of the men had rifles with them for hunting, but most of the rifles and handguns were packed away in the backs of the wagons. Before leaving Kansas they had discussed defensive procedures among themselves, and the consensus had been that they would be safer once they entered the territory if they weren't armed. That way, they figured, the Indians would not regard them as a threat. So far their reasoning had been correct. But that was because they had only encountered reasoning Indians. They had not planned on meeting a renegade like Tom Blue.

Tom Blue, his blood running hot, urged his horse after one of the burning wagons. He could see the horses, their nostrils flared, their eyes wild with panic, running at a full gallop as they pulled the wagon at breakneck speed across the plains. The burning wagon trailed a long plume of smoke and flames. With a shout of glee, the Comanche leaped from the back of his horse onto the wagon. Working against the encroaching flames, he began pushing the contents of the wagon out onto the ground, leaving a trail of goods behind him: trunks, a chair, a table, pots and pans, a child's doll.

The Indians who were riding with Tom split up into three groups, each group chasing down one of the burning wagons. As a result of their diverted attention, the other, undamaged, wagons began pulling away to safety, and even the men and women who had abandoned the burning wagons were able to find shelter with their fleeing neighbors.

Except for the Hope family.

When Laurel's father gave the order to jump and ran toward the other wagons, Laurel was horrified to see her little sister running in the wrong direction.

"Penny! Penny, this way!" Laurel called to her, but the little girl, who was only four years old, was so panic-stricken she didn't know what she was doing.

Laurel's mother started after the little girl, then her father started after both of them. The mother and father had ran no more than a few steps until both of them were cut down by gunfire.

"Mama! Papa!" Laurel screamed. She put her hand to her mouth in horror as she saw her parents go down. Then, because Penny was still running in the wrong direction, Laurel went after her. She finally caught up to the terrified youngster, then turned to go back. That was when she saw that the wagons, pulled at full speed by frightened teams, were already a quarter of a mile away. There was no way she could catch up with them.

"Wait!" she called. "Wait for me!"

Her entreaties were too late, too thin to be heard against the roar of wind, rolling wheels, squeaking harness, pounding hooves, and heart-thumping pulse. Horrified, Laurel watched the wagons roll away to leave her behind. She grabbed her little sister and darted over to a small bush to hide and watch.

Tom Blue jumped off the burning wagon, shouting with joy as he watched the other wagons flee. Some of the men on the wagons had managed to fire at him, but it was as if he had been impervious to their bullets. He leaped onto the back of his pony, singing his victory song.

Hiding behind the bush, Laurel held Penny against her skirt, shushing her to keep her quiet. She looked at the burning wagons and at the treasures of the families that now lay scattered across the plains. She saw the grandfather's clock that had been her mother's most proud possession lying smashed on the ground. It had come over from Germany, was handed down to Laurel's mother. Her mother had told her how it would one day be hers, and then her children's and her children's' children. One hundred years from now, her mother had said, the Hope family would gather around the grandfather's clock and tell its story. But the story of the clock had ended here on the Oklahoma plains. Laurel looked over at her parents. Both were full of bullet holes, lying motionless in the grass.

Though she wanted to cry for them, she had no time for grief because suddenly one of the Indians started riding toward her. The Indian, who was not only painted but had a hideous scar on his face, brandished a tomahawk as he rode toward her. He leaned far out to one side of the horse so he could get low enough for the blow. Laurel screamed and tried to jerk Penny out of the way. She was too late. Even as she held her sister in her hands, the tomahawk smashed into the blond curls of the little girl and Laurel was splashed with blood and brain matter from her sister's head.

Laurel fell into a deep swoon and sank into unconsciousness.

Jim Early stayed with the Black Maria while Ned and the other two deputies rode toward the sound of the gunfire. He continued to work on the wheel, pulling the broken spokes out. He discovered there were two of them, and he began fitting the replacement spokes in. He had just fit the first one into place and was starting on the second when he heard the rumbling thunder of pounding hooves. He looked in the direction of the sound and saw several Indians riding by at a full gallop. One of them was carrying a chair, another a small table, while a third was wearing a bright yellow jacket and a fur cap. Jim realized it must be booty the Indians had stolen from the wagon train.

The Indians saw him at the same time as he saw them, and they started in his direction, yelling and barking their cries of challenge. Here was one more victim for their blood lust.

An arrow came arching from the direction of the Indians. It hit the ground about five feet away from Early. Three more came flying toward him, two of them burrowing into the ground, the third clanging off the bars of the wagon. A white puff of smoke told him they were firing rifles as well.

Jim pulled his rifle from the scabbard by the wagon seat, then dropped to one knee and, with arrows raining around him, calmly took aim. His rifle barked once and an Indian fell from his horse, the chair he was carrying flying up into the air. Jim levered in a fresh round and fired a second time. The Indian in the yellow jacket pitched over his mount's head, and the remaining Indians turned, then galloped away. That was when Jim saw that one of them had a girl with him. The girl was lying across the horse's withers in front of the Indian. Jim couldn't tell by looking if she was alive or dead. She was belly down on the horse and not moving, but he assumed she must be alive . . . otherwise the Indians would have left her.

"So, you've added kidnapping to your list have you?" Jim mused. "Pretty soon, Mr. Blue, there won't be any crimes left you haven't done."

"She's sixteen," Abner Poindexter was saying. "She's a pretty little thing, about the same size as Mrs. Cummins, there, blond hair, blue eyes."

The wagons had stopped their mad dash and were back on their original trail. They were camped now, while the men of the train helped the survivors sift through their burned-out wagons to gather the items the Indians had left behind. They also found the bodies of the Hope family, all except Laurel. Jim had already reported seeing a girl on one of the Indian horses.

"What'll them savages do to her, Marshal?" Poindexter asked.

"Maybe just hold her for ransom," Ned said, sparing them his darkest thoughts. "Until her family pays to have her released."

"The girl ain't got no family left," Poindexter explained. "What folks her mama had left are over in Europe. Her papa was an orphan. That girl ain't got a soul who even knows about her, let alone cares for her."

"Marshal, Abner, we're about to have the buryin' of Mr. and Mrs. Hope and little Penny," Matt Parker called, interrupting the conversation at that moment. "Would you like to come?"

"Yes," Ned said.

Ned and his deputies joined the others from the wagon train to stand by the three graves that had been newly opened. One of the graves was pitifully small, giving stark evidence of the size of the victim. The three bodies had been sewn into canvas shrouds, and as the marshals and the others stood there, the bodies of the Hope family were gently lowered into the holes. The wagon master said a few words over them, then a couple of men started closing the graves. The dirt made a poignant, heart-wrenching sound as it fell on the canvas. Ned thought of the lonely graves like this that were scattered all over the West, marking the pioneer trails of the last forty years.

After the train set up camp for the night, spits and stewpans were soon put to use, and the air became laden with the aromatic smells of cooking meat. Ned and his men were invited to supper, and they accepted the invitation gratefully.

"Tell me, Marshal," Matt Parker said over the meal that night. "This Indian who attacked us . . . you say his name is Blue? Tom Blue?"

"Yes."

"Well, if he's a war chief leading a bunch of Indians on the warpath, why don't the government set the army against him, 'stead of just a U.S. Marshal and a couple of deputies. Why, you've come out here after him with a jail wagon like he weren't no more trouble than a common criminal."

"He is a common criminal, Mr. Parker," Ned told him. "War chief? War chiefs don't make war against four-year-old girls. To call the army out against him would be to pay him respect ... and to dishonor all the other Indians, those who are living peacefully, and even those we've had to fight from time to time."

"But if he gets enough wild young bucks to follow him, how do you ever plan to catch him? You have only three men with you."

"What do you think about that, Jim?" Ned asked, smiling at his deputy.

Jim Early squirted a stream of tobacco toward the fire. "I reckon we'll get the job done," he said.

Showdown at Comanche Butte

Chapter 7

NED AND HIS DEPUTIES tracked the band of renegades for the next four days. Late in the afternoon of the fourth day they saw a thin line of smoke spiraling above the horizon. It wasn't the kind of smoke you might get from a campfire—it was too big for that— and it wasn't smoke from an incidental brush fire because it wasn't spread out enough for that. There was only one thing that could cause smoke like that: a cabin or a structure of some sort.

By the time they reached the site and confirmed the source of the smoke, the cabin had burned all the way to the ground, with only the mud chimney still standing. A man and woman, with smoke blackened faces, stood in front of the smoking pile of embers, looking at what had Iseen their home. They glanced around as Ned and the others arrived.

"Did you see them?" the man asked.

Ned indicated the burned house. "You mean the ones who did this?"

"Yeah. A bunch of thievin', dirty Indians."

"Comanche?"

The man ran his hand through his hair. "I think so," he said. "Truth to tell, I'm not all that good at pickin' one out from the other. I seen the one leadin' 'em, though. I can sure describe him if I ever have to."

"Short, muscular, got a scar right here?"

"Yes," the man answered. He looked at Ned and the others, saw the Black Maria. "Sounds like you know him."

"Yeah, I know him. We've been on his trail." Ned introduced himself and his deputies.

"The name's Frank Dupree," the farmer said. "This here's my wife, Martha."

"Want to tell us what happened here, Mr. Dupree?" Ned asked.

"Well, they come in here this mornin'," Dupree explained. "I seen 'em just after sunup. At first I thought they was just passin' through, maybe wanted to trade a little. Indians do that here, sometimes. They'll maybe trade a fresh-kilt deer for some coffee, tobacco, or the like. Truth to tell, I don't mind them comin' aroun'. Fresh deer meat's a treat after nothin' but beans an' pork for a month or so, an' I don't get much time to get out an' hunt. But these here Indians went straight to the corral, started cuttin' out my horses."

"What'd you do?" Jim asked.

"Hell, I run into the house an' got my rifle . . . started shootin' at 'em. I run 'em away, but they stood off a ways and shot fire arrows into the house until they had it burnin' good. Once they had it smokin', why they hauled off an' left. Me an' the wife tried to put it out, but it was too late, the fire had done took hold."

"Everythin' we had got burnt up in that fire, Marshal," Mrs. Dupree said. She could have been in her late twenties or late forties, Ned had no way of knowing. She showed the effects of a life of hard labor. Ned had seen many women just like her in this country. They were the real builders of the West. "You say you been after them heathens?" she added.

"Yes'm," Ned answered.

"I pray that you catch them."

"We'll get them, Mrs. Dupree," Ned promised. "You can count on that."

"What will you do now?" Dan asked the settler. "They ain't no question what I'm gonna do. I got my crop in," Dupree answered. "I'm goin' to stay an' work it. Me an' Martha slept out on the groun' when we first come out here four years ago, I reckon we can do it again. I'll have us a nice soddy up before cold weather sets in again. I'd like to see the heathen bastards try an' burn that."

"We're going on to Fort Supply," Ned said. "Anything we can do for you while we're there?"

"Just send them heathens to the happy huntin' ground is all I want."

"I don't know how happy it'll be when they get there," Ned said. "But I promise you, we'll send them on their way."

Established in November of 1868, Fort Supply was located on a low, sandy bottom between the North Canadian River and Wolf Creek, very near their junction. Commanded by Col. Alfred Sulley, the post had been built in connection with Gen. Phil Sheridan's winter campaign against the Cheyenne, Kiowa, and other Plains Indian tribes. Its continued existence was relative to the necessity of providing protection for people on cattle drives and those coming through on wagon trains.

Originally a tent settlement, it had by now been transformed into a community of solid structures. The officers' quarters were adobe, but most of the other buildings, barracks, shops, stables, the guardhouse, and post trader's store were constructed of logs chinked with a mixture of mud, sand, and lime.

When the Black Maria and its outriders rolled through the main gate, they were passed in by a private who was standing ceremonial, if not actual, guard. Half a league away a company of men marched on the parade quadrangle, and the barking orders of their drill sergeant drifted across the sun-baked ground to Ned's ears. Closer by, a Gatling gun crew was going through its unlimbering practice, while two men, under guard, were policing up the area as punishment for their drunken excesses of the day before.

A shavetail lieutenant, his epaulets bare, reported to them. Stopping just short of saluting, he came to attention.

"Sir, you are Marshal Remington?"

"I am."

"One of our scouts reported that you were in the area. Col. Sulley's compliments, sir, and he asks if you and your deputies would join him for supper?"

"Tell the colonel we would consider it a privilege," Ned replied.

Hanging ollas, which were great clay pots of water, made the dining room pleasantly cool by the simple process of evaporation. Dressed in full-dress uniform, strikers, as the colonel's orderlies were called, served the meal of roast beef, baked potatoes, and minted peas. Mrs. Sulley, a woman of mature beauty, and her two very pretty teenaged daughters were dressed as if attending a ball. They hovered about, making certain the correct silver was put out, the finest china was in place, even the colonel, a tall, slim man with mutton-chop whiskers, was in his "mess-dress" uniform.

Lt. Ferguson, the shavetail who had greeted Ned and the others, was also present, as was his wife, a beautiful young woman who had just arrived on the post three weeks ago. Lt. Ferguson was the colonel's aide and, as such, was present for the supper.

Ned and his deputies were wearing the same clothes they rode in with and were feeling a little self-conscious about the dress of the others. Col. Sulley noticed the look of discomfort on Ned's face, and he chuckled softly.

"Don't pay any attention to all the fal-do-rah of our dress," he said. "Life out here gets pretty boring . . . especially for the ladies. As a result, we sometimes go out of our way to turn the slightest thing into a social event. I'm sure you gentlemen would have been just as satisfied by seating yourselves at the men's mess. But please allow us our indulgences."

"That's quite all right," Ned said. "If you don't mind us sticking out like sore thumbs at your party, we don't mind being here."

"Umm, my compliments to your cook, madam," Dan Norling said as he tasted the beef. "I'd say it was marinated in a good red wine and seasoned with thyme and marjoram."

"Oh, are you a cook, Mr. Norling?" Mrs. Sulley asked in surprise.

"No," Kurt answered for him. "Dan is not just a cook. . . . He is a chef!"

"A chef? My, how fascinating! We simply must exchange recipes."

The conversation drifted along pleasantly for several more minutes, then it turned to the business at hand. Col. Sulley asked who they were after.

"Tom Blue," Ned answered. "Do you know him?" Sulley filled his pipe and began tamping down the bowl. "Yes," he answered, "I know him. In fact, after the Doomey ranch massacre, I tried to get permission to mount an expedition against him, but headquarters wouldn't approve it. I'm badly under strength here, Marshal. If I take to the field in pursuit of one renegade Indian, even one who is followed by as many as Tom Blue, some others might see that as an opportunity to go on the warpath."

"That is something to think about," Ned agreed. "Yes, I suppose it is. Still, it gets damn boring out here, month after month. A little field duty would be good for the men. But you are going after him with just the four of you?"

"Yes."

Sulley lit his pipe then and puffed on it until his head was encircled with a wreath of blue smoke.

"Well, I tell you true, Marshal, you're going to have your hands full. Blue has gathered himself quite a band of Comanches."

"What's got him worked up?" Jim asked.

"There's a man out here trading illegal whiskey to the Indians for all the guns, gold, and goods the Indians can steal. He's the one behind Blue."

"Nate Luckless?"

"Yes. Do you know him?" the colonel replied. "No. But I do have a warrant to serve on him,"

"His name is Luckless," Lt. Ferguson spat, "but his name should be Worthless."

Col. Sulley chuckled. "Jerry had a run-in with Mr. Luckless when he was the sutler here."

"Luckless was your sutler? I didn't know that," Ned said.

"He's a most unpleasant man," Mrs. Sulley put in. "I was very glad when he lost his sutler's license. I didn't even like to go into the place when he was here."

"Jerry caught him cheating the men," Col. Sulley said. "He brought it to my attention, and I had the man removed."

"I don't suppose he took too kindly to that," Ned suggested.

"Not at all. Matter of fact, he swore that he'd get even," Col. Sulley said. "I guess that's what he's now doing, goading a renegade on like that."

"Not counting the Doomey ranch, where we have no eyewitnesses to confirm or deny Tom Blue's involvement, that renegade has already killed four that I know of," Ned said. "He killed a cattleman and stole his herd, then he attacked a wagon train, killed a man, his wife, and a little girl."

"He burned out the Dupree farm," Kurt added. "Yes, and he kidnapped a young girl, only sixteen," Jim said. "She was the only one left alive from the family of wagon train settlers he killed."

"Oh, the poor child," Mrs. Sulley gasped. "She is in his hands? To think of one of my own dear, sweet children in the hands of savages." The Sulley girls and Lt. Ferguson's wife, herself not much older than the Sulley girls, shivered involuntarily.

"I do hope you get the girl back, Marshal," Lt. Ferguson said.

"We'll get her," Ned said grimly. Left unsaid was the girl's condition once they found her. He thought of his own daughter back in Missouri. She was still suffering from the horror she had gone through. Would Laurel Hope wind up being like his daughter?

"This fella, Luckless. What does he look like?" Jim asked.

"You can't forget him once you meet him," Sulley said. "He's a big bear of a man, bushy beard, but bald-headed."

"Maybe that's why he feels safe with the Indians," Dan teased. "No scalp to take."

"And if ever there was a white man's scalp I would like to see as some Comanche's trophy, it would be his," Sulley said.

"Do you have any idea where Luckless has his trading post?"

"No, not really," Sulley said.

"Perhaps Mrs. Miller, sir," Lt. Ferguson suggested.

"Yes," Sulley agreed. "Yes, I hadn't thought of her."

"Who is Mrs. Miller?"

"Verity Miller," Sulley explained. "She's a widow, lives about twenty miles northwest of here. Her husband was a prairie farmer, killed last year by a group of renegades. Always thought Tom Blue might have had something to do with that, too, but Mrs. Miller hid in the root cellar and didn't get a good look at any of them, so we can't prove it."

"I took the patrol out that found her," Ferguson went on. "Mrs. Miller said her husband had told her about an illegal trading post, one that was selling whiskey to the Indians. He planned to report it to us; She figured that might be why the farm was attacked and her husband killed. She blames it on Luckless."

"And she knows where the trading post is?"

"She has a pretty good idea," Ferguson said. "I wanted to take a party out to find it and close it down."

"But headquarters wouldn't approve it," Sulley completed, "so nothing has been done."

"I don't need headquarters' approval," Ned said. "We'll find the place."

"What will you do when you find it?" Ferguson wanted to know.

"We'll look it over quietly for a while. If he's furnishing Blue with whiskey, Blue won't stay away too long before he comes back. When he does, we'll be able to get both of them."

"If you do that, you'll probably stop ninety percent of the things that have been going on around here," Col. Sulley suggested. "Good luck to you."

"Oh, Colonel, if you can spare them, I'd like to draw a few rations," Ned asked. "I can pay for them."

"Sure, you're welcome to what we have. Mostly beans and bacon."

"We got in some canned peaches," Ferguson added. "They aren't bad."

"I appreciate it. We'll draw them first thing in the morning," Ned said.

Ned, Dan, Kurt, and Jim rode out of Fort Supply the next morning as the last notes of the bugler's reveille hung in the air behind them, and the Stars and Stripes was raised briskly to the top of the flagpole.

The men had spent the night in one of the barracks. They hadn't wanted to insult the colonel by refusing his offer, but in truth they were used to sleeping outside and would probably have enjoyed a better rest outdoors than by listening to half a dozen soldiers snore the whole night through. However, they had enjoyed a good meal the night before and they did refill their saddlebags with rations, including the treat of a few cans of peaches. And best of all, they had a lead as to how to find Tom Blue.

Follow the whiskey trail, Ned thought. At its end they would find their quarry.

Chapter 8

VERITY MILLER LEANED on the hoe and looked out over the field of com. Already head high, it was coming along quite nicely, and she felt a justifiable sense of pride in having put it in all by herself.

"What do you think of your city woman now, Clyde?" she asked quietly. Verity brushed an errant strand of hair back from her forehead and thought of the dead husband she had known for less than a year.

Verity had been teaching school in St. Louis when she saw the advertisement in the *St. Louis Globe.*

WANTED, a Christian woman of child-bearing years, to be my wife. Must be willing to share a life of hard work on a farm. She doesn't have to be pretty.

Verity thought she fit the description perfectly. She was a Christian woman of child-bearing years, she was willing to work hard, and she wasn't pretty. The only problem was she had never lived on a farm, but she was willing to learn.

Verity answered the advertisement and two weeks later took the train to Kansas City, where Clyde met her, rushed her to the preacher, and married her before she even had time to change into the dress she had bought for the wedding.

She found out why he had been in such a hurry a short time later when they went straight from the church to join a wagon train that was going into the Oklahoma territory.

"When we get there, we'll have a whole section of land to work, Verity," Clyde had told her. "A team of mules, a cow, seed corn and wheat, a plow. It's a steel plow too, not one of those cast-iron things. And on top of that, I've got me the finest new wife a fella could ever want."

"Well, Clyde Miller, it's nice to know that I'm mentioned in the same sentence as your steel plow," Verity had teased.

"What?" He was thrown into confusion.

"Never mind, Clyde. I was only joshing you."

"Oh. Well, it's not only me who has everything needed to get a good start. Back there under the canvas I got some nice things for you, too."

Verity thought of curtains, tablecloths, bedspreads, a few things soft and pretty, and she felt a warmth toward this stranger who was her husband. "Tell me about them," she said.

"Well, I bought you a stove, a tin wash boiler, two iron pots, a teakettle, two pie pans, a steamer, a coffeepot, a coal-oil can, a gridiron, four tin cups, four plates, and four forks. Right now that's in case we got company, but it's also for when we get our family started. Aside from all that, I bought you a washbasin, a pepper box, a lamp, and a bucket." As he finished the inventory, he smiled at her, waiting for a word of praise.

Verity's initial reaction was one of disappointment. While he was reciting the litany of her possessions, she was waiting for him to say he had bought something, anything, even if frivolous, to bring some gentleness to the life before her. Then she scolded herself. She realized that she didn't need anything frivolous, but she did need the things he had mentioned. She suspected that within a month of being a settler's wife she wouldn't trade one of the things he had mentioned.

"It sounds wonderful," she said, and he beamed proudly, started to put his arm around her, thought better of it, and pulled it back until she leaned against him to tell him that it was all right.

For the seven weeks it took them to get there, Clyde regaled her with stories of their section of land, and by the time they arrived she was very anxious to see their new home. But there was little to see, not only because the house hadn't been built yet, but because it was the middle of night when they arrived. The moon was but a slender crescent, shedding little light on the rolling prairie. There were no hills or trees or even rocks to fix in her mind, only a vast darkness stretching away from her.

Using the North Star to get his alignment, Clyde started laying out the walls of their sod house that very night, while she gathered buffalo chips for the fire and made dough for tomorrow's bread. From that moment until the day Clyde was killed, they worked from an hour before sunup to an hour after sundown every day . . . and she wouldn't have traded one minute of it.

They never got the family started. Less than one year after they moved into their "soddy" they were attacked by a roving band of Indians. Clyde put Verity in the root cellar and tried to fight them off, but he was killed. When it was all over, one of the Indians came into the cellar and rummaged around, finally leaving with three jars of pickles Verity had put up. The Indians didn't know there was a woman living in the place. Verity was hiding behind a barrel in the comer, and the Indians never saw her.

Verity was afraid to look up lest she be seen, so she didn't see any of them. She could hear them talking among themselves though, and one of them said the name Luckless. She was certain of that. . . . the name had stood out in bold relief against the stream of Indian talk. Luckless, she knew, was the trader Clyde had told her was selling whiskey to the Indians. She also knew that Clyde had threatened to report him to the military authorities if he didn't stop. She believed with all her heart that Luckless had her husband killed.

After Verity buried Clyde, she thought about returning to Kansas City or St. Louis. But the crop was nearly ready for harvest so she decided to stay. She hired someone to help her get the com and wheat in, and found that the labor took up most of the profit. She was a quick learner though, and she watched everything the hired man did. She decided right then that she would stay on, get the seed out and the crop in by herself from then on. And that was just what she was doing.

When she first saw the men approaching, she thought about going back to the house for the rifle. But there was something about them, about the steady, measured progress made by the three mounted men and a strange- looking wagon, that made her think she had nothing to fear. She went up to the house, filled a wash pan with water and freshened up a bit. It wasn't often she got company, and she didn't want to greet them looking like a field hand.

Laurel had been Tom Blue's captive for nearly a week. In that time she had seen no one other than the Indians who were part of the band. She had come to believe that they were operating outside the limits, not only of white man's law, but Indian law as well. She harbored hope that she might be rescued, if not by whites, then by Indians. She looked every day, hoping to see someone, anyone, as she believed her lot could only improve.

Though she had not been physically abused, she lived in mortal fear of the time the Indians would have her way with her. They had moved from campsite to campsite, never staying in one place longer than a single night. At first she had ridden double with one or another of the Indians, but finally they put her on her own horse with her hands tied.

They didn't eat during the day. Only at night, after a long day of travel, would they take time for a meal. Generally it would be a rabbit or prairie chicken or antelope meat. Laurel would have to sit quietly, waiting for the others to eat their fill so she could eat what was left. Sometimes there was little more than the marrow of the bones to sustain her, but whatever it was, Laurel took it, hanging on to life with a fierce tenacity.

On this, the sixth night of her captivity, Laurel sat by the fire, dirtier than she had ever been in her life, her hair hanging in matted strands, her dress tattered and torn, her fingernails broken, as wild-looking as any creature who ever wandered the plains. If a white person saw her now, she believed, they wouldn't even recognize her as one of their kind.

For the first two days the Indians had spoken only in their own language. Then, three days after she was captured, the leader of the group spoke English to her. He identified himself as Tom Blue. She had tried many times to engage him in conversation, but he never spoke except to give orders. Once he told her that women should keep silent.

Laurel watched as Tom Blue wolfed down the rabbit. A piece of it was hanging from his lips; his face shone with the rabbit's grease.

"What is going to happen to me?" she asked. She had asked the same question many times, only to be greeted by silence. She had no reason to believe this time would be any different, but she had to try.

"We sell you," Blue answered.

Laurel was shocked! He actually spoke to her. He actually answered her question.

"Sell me? Sell me to who?"

"We sell you to white man."

"A white man?" She was very excited now. "You are going to sell me to a white man?"

"Maybe he will pay much for you."

"Oh, I understand. You are going to make a white man pay a ransom for my return, is that it?" She breathed a sigh of relief. "Good, good. Whatever ransom you demand, I will find some way to repay him."

"You will pay him?" Blue asked.

"Yes, I will."

Blue laughed aloud. "I have heard that among the whites, men pay for such things," he said. "I have never heard of a woman paying." He made a circle of the thumb and forefinger on his left hand, then stuck his right forefinger in it and moved it back and forth. It wasn't a gesture that Laurel understood, but it made her uneasy. When the Indians laughed about it, it was a low, guttural laugh that made her flesh crawl with goosebumps.

Later that night, Laurel was awakened from a fitful sleep by the unmistakable sound of a white man. Or, more correctly, white men, because when she sat up she saw two men talking with Blue. One of them was tall and thin, with a prominent Adam's apple and large eyes; the other was shorter, stocky, with a bushy mustache.

"Oh, thank God you are here!"

"Well now, Frank," the tall, thin man said. "Lookie here, would you? What ye think o' this? A white girl runnin' with these here savages."

"Cain't be no decent girl," Frank replied, stroking his mustache.

"Oh, but I am," Laurel tried to explain. "My clothes, my hair, I haven't had a chance to clean up and—"

"'Cause iffen she was a decent girl, she'd be dead. She would'a already kilt herself."

The tall thin one laughed and rubbed himself gleefully. "Well, now, ain't it just our luck we'uns found us a girl out here who ain't decent?"

With a sinking heart, Laurel realized that she hadn't been saved. She had merely been thrust from one danger to another. She had thought that leaving the Indians who captured her could only mean an improvement in her lot. As the tall, thin man began pulling at her dress, she realized how wrong she had been.

"Mrs. Miller, I want to thank you for setting a dinner table for my deputies and me," Ned said.

"I'm glad for the company, Marshal Remington," Verity said. "And I'm glad someone is doing something about that man, Luckless."

"You've been a big help by telling us where to find his trading post."

"I hope it's still there," Verity said. "My husband told me it was at the junction of Gypsum Creek and the North Canadian, but that was last summer. It could be that he's moved."

"If he has, we'll find him," Ned promised.

As they left the house and mounted for their ride, Jim, who was sitting on the seat of the Black Maria, looked out over the cornfield.

"You've done a fine job of runnin' this place alone," he said.

Verity sighed. "I suppose so. But it does seem hollow and empty. I know wishing is a futile gesture, but I wish Clyde and I had had a chance to get our family started. If I just had a child to ease my loneliness . . ." She let the sentence trail off, then, realizing what she had said, blushed mightily. "I'm a foolish woman," she said. "Pay no attention to me."

Suddenly Ned had an idea. "Mrs. Miller, you recall the girl we told you about? The one who was captured from the wagon train?"

"Yes."

"I was just thinking. Her family is dead. When we find her there's going to be no place for her—"

"Oh, Marshal, yes!" Verity said, interrupting before Ned could even finish his thought. "I would love to take her! I could give her a home, I could even start her education. And she could be company for me.

"You understand that she's been through quite an ordeal. I'm not at all sure . . ." He stopped and thought of his own Katy, then took a deep breath and went on. "I'm not sure she'll even have her wits about her."

"She'll need a place to go one way or the other, won't she?"

"Well, yes."

"Then she'll come here," Verity said.

Ned leaned forward and patted the neck of his horse. "You're a good woman, Verity Miller," he said.

Verity's smile warmed him, but brought a sad tug to his heart as well. A woman's smile. It did things to a man.

At that moment, he missed Katy more than ever. He tried vainly to swallow the lump in his throat.

Chapter 9

THEY FOUND THE TRADING POST just before daylight at the confluence of the shallow North Canadian River and the dry Gypsum Creek. The creek wasn't always dry, as evidenced by the bed which was marked by a thin earthen crust. The crust had formed since the water last ran, only to bake and crack in the sun. Preserved in the crust were the tracks of a coyote, as fresh and clear as if the animal had passed by only this morning.

A gulley shot off from Gypsum Creek to pass about fifty yards in front of the trading post, and it was there that Ned had Jim take the Black Maria and horses to keep them out of sight. Somewhat closer to the trading post was an outcropping of granite boulders, and using them for cover, the men were able to keep the trading post under observation.

Just after sunup an Indian man and his woman arrived. The Indian man sat down with his back against the side of the building and went to sleep. The woman, who had been carrying a bundle, sat down also, but she started grinding corn into meal.

Half an hour later, a large, bearded, bald-headed man came out of the building. He relieved himself uphill from the woman and she had to move to avoid the yellow stream of water that began trickling toward her.

"That's Luckless," Dan said.

"*Ja*" Kurt answered.

"Sociable sort of gent, isn't he?" Jim observed.

Luckless laughed when he saw the Indian woman get up and leave.

"What's the matter, 'fraid to get a little piss in yer cornmeal?" he asked. "What do ye' want, Artichoke?" he asked the Indian man.

"Whiskey."

"Oh, ye' want whiskey, do ye'? What do ye' have to trade?"

Artichoke pointed to the woman. "Cornmeal," he said.

"Cornmeal? What the hell am I going to do with cornmeal? Ye' want whiskey, yer goin' to have to bring me somethin' I can use." He made a rubbing motion with his thumb and forefinger. "Money . . . gold, things like that."

"No have."

"No, and ye' ain't gonna have it long as ye' sit around on yer dead ass an' let yer woman do all yer work. Why don't ye' join up with Tom Blue?"

Artichoke shook his head. "Tom Blue is bad Indian."

"'Tom Blue is bad Indian,' " Luckless mocked. "So are ye' if ye' drink whiskey. Don't ye' know it's against the law for an Indian to drink whiskey? They'll hang ye' for that as quick as they will anything else, so ye' might as well take what ye' can."

"No," Artichoke said.

"No? Well, then get on, get outta here," Luckless said, making a waving motion with his hand. "It don't do note no good to have yer kind around. I'm lookin' for Tom Blue to come in today."

"Thank you, Mr. Luckless," Ned said quietly. "That's just what we wanted to hear."

Artichoke said something to the Indian woman, and she stopped grinding com, folded everything up into the blanket, and followed him as he walked away. Ned was glad to see them leave; he wanted them out of the way when the action started.

It was nearly noon when Kurt shook Ned awake from a short nap. "We have company," he said.

"Tom Blue?"

"Ja. There are two more besides."

"Let them get inside."

Ned and the others waited until Tom Blue and the two Comanches with him were inside the building. Then, crouched over and moving swiftly, they darted toward the building. Pausing just for a moment to look around, Ned kicked open the door and the marshals burst inside.

"United States Marshals!" Ned shouted. "Everybody stay right where you are."

"What the hell?" Luckless shouted. Tom Blue started toward the door and Ned dived after him, knocking him to the floor.

While Ned and Tom Blue were fighting on the floor, an old Indian man came inside.

"Get out of here!" Jim roared at him, and Luckless, seeing the opportunity, grabbed a pistol from beneath the counter. He squeezed the trigger, not so much in the hope of hitting someone, as in creating confusion. The gun went off and a large puff of white smoke billowed out into the room.

Dan fired at the smoke, but Luckless had already moved, and the smoke from Dan's discharge merely added to the fog in the room. Using the dense smoke as a cover, Luckless pushed through a side door, leaped onto the back of a horse, and galloped away.

"Damn!" Jim said. "The sonofabitch is getting away!" Jim, Dan, and Kurt ran to the doorway but Luckless knew the terrain well and had already reached the safety of a shielding outcropping of rocks. To make matters worse, while they were concerned about Luckless, the two remaining Comanches escaped as well. Only Tom Blue was firmly in their grasp ... or more literally, in Ned's grasp. Ned stood up and jerked the Indian to his feet.

"Where's the girl you took?" Ned asked.

The Indian spit in Ned's face, and Ned retaliated by sending a whistling punch to the mouth. Tom Blue went down like a sack of meal, out cold.

Ned paused for a moment to get his breath, then he pointed at the Indian's prostrate form.

"Jim, you drag his ass out to the wagon," he said. "Dan, Kurt, let's go after the others."

Ned and his deputies ran to their horses and hauled themselves up into the saddles. They didn't see Luckless, but they did see the two Comanches. They set out in hot pursuit.

The reason the two Indians had not made a clean getaway was that they were leading a third horse. It, too, had a rider ... a girl.

"Ned! Do you see?" Dan called.

"It must be Laurel Hope," Ned replied. He, like the other two, had drawn his pistol but hadn't fired. "Don't shoot. You might hit her."

Suddenly the third horse was turned loose by the Indians and sent to gallop off on its own. The girl's hands were still tied and she had no way of controlling her horse. Ned and his deputies did exactly what the Indians figured they would do, they started after the girl, thus giving them the chance to get away.

It was half a minute before Ned was able to catch up to the Indian pony that was running away with the girl. He reached out and pulled the girl off the horse, then stopped and set her gently on the ground. He hopped down and began untying her.

"Are you all right, Laurel?" he asked.

The girl looked at him in surprise. "You know my name?"

"Yes. I'm U.S. Marshal Ned Remington. We've been looking for you."

"You're not going to hurt me?" Her eyes were bright with fear.

"Hurt you? No, of course not. You're safe now."

"The others . . . they hurt me."

"Don't you worry, little miss," Dan said soothingly. "Those heathens will pay for what they did."

"Not the Indians," Laurel said. "The white men!"

Now it was Ned's turn to be surprised.

"Did you say white men?"

"Yes. Yesterday two white men came to the camp. They gave the Indians whiskey, and I thought it was to buy my freedom. I was wrong. It was so they could ... they . . . " She stopped.

"You don't have to go on, miss," Ned said. "I understand."

The girl, as if realizing that she could finally let go, began to cry, and Ned took her into his arms. He held her for a long time, letting her tears soak into his shoulder. He knew that the others were getting away, but it didn't matter. Right now this was more important than chasing them. Besides, he had Tom Blue. He had the idea that he wouldn't really have to chase the others. They would come after him.

Jim indicated that Laurel should get up on the seat beside him for the trip back. She put her foot on one of the spokes of the wheel to climb up when she saw Tom Blue locked up inside the wagon. She let out a gasp of fear, then pulled back.

"It's all right, girl," Jim said. "He's locked up tighter'n a drum. There's no way he can hurt you."

Despite Jim's assurances, Ned had to lift her up onto the seat, and she sat there, curled up in fear, withdrawing inside herself. The strength the girl had used to survive had also helped her maintain her sanity. Now that she was in no physical danger and no longer had to fight to survive, she let go. What she didn't realize was that she was still in great emotional danger, for without the strength to hold her together, her mind was beginning to slip away.

Ned knew exactly what she was going through, what was happening to her. He had seen it all before in his own daughter and it was almost too painful for him to go through again.

Several times during the next few hours of their journey Ned would drop back to ride alongside the wagon for a while. Each time he tried to start a conversation with Laurel, tried to reach inside of her, to hold her together. Sometimes he would point out a patch of pretty wildflowers, other times an interesting rock formation, anything that might draw her out. He was unsuccessful in every attempt. Finally he decided that the best thing to do would be to confront her directly. He switched places with Jim, driving the wagon himself while Jim rode ahead on the horse.

"Laurel, I know what you are going through right now."

Laurel stared straight ahead.

"You feel unclean, like you could take a bath in a river with a whole washtub of lye soap and you still wouldn't come clean. You feel guilty because you are alive and your family is dead. You think, somehow, that you've sinned, and you feel like people will be able to see it all in your face from now on."

It worked. He reached her, and Laurel looked at him as if shocked that he could understand what she was feeling. Her brow wrinkled, and her eyes opened up windows that let him see all the way to her soul.

"You're wondering how I know all this, aren't you?" Ned asked, seizing the advantage. He recognized that he had made some inroads, and it was all he could do to keep from shouting for joy. Maybe it wasn't too late.

Laurel didn't speak, but she did nod her head yes. She was, at last, communicating.

"I know because it happened to me."

"It . . .it happened to you?" Laurel said, finally speaking. "I don't understand. How?"

"Because it happened to my daughter," Ned said. "And when she hurts I can feel it as much as if it was my own hurt."

"Where is your daughter now?"

"She's being looked after in a convent back in Missouri. I didn't say the right words, do the right things, and she's still hurting . . . still living what happened to her. She's afraid of life. I don't want that to happen to you, Laurel. You're a young girl with a whole life in front of you. I want you to put everything that happened behind you."

"How can I do that?"

"By starting fresh."

"How can I start fresh?" Laurel asked. Tears welled up in her eyes now, and they were tears of grief. This was good, too. It was her first opportunity to show grief, or even to feel it. "My family is dead and I have no place to go."

"Yes, you do. There's a woman near here, a good woman, named Verity Miller. You and Mrs. Miller have something in common. She lost her husband last year to the same man who killed your family. She's living on a farm, making a go of it, and she's all alone. She could use some company . . . and some help. I'm going to take you there."

"What if . . ." Laurel started, then she let the words hang.

"What?"

"What if she doesn't want me?"

"She wants you. She told me to bring you by."

"I don't know. Maybe we won't like each other. We've never met; we don't know anything about each other."

"Well, that may be," Ned said softly. "But she's a good woman, you're a decent girl. You need each other. If there is a problem, you'll work it out."

The conversation stopped then, and Laurel was silent for a long time. However, Ned could sense the difference in the silence. This wasn't the silence of withdrawal…this was the silence of contemplation. He had given the girl something to think about, and he was pleased to see that she was doing just that.

It was late in the afternoon when they reached Verity Miller's farm. After having put in a full day in the fields, Verity was now baking biscuits. She was wearing an apron and dusting flour off her hands as she came out to greet her visitors. She saw the young girl on the Black Maria, sitting on the seat beside Jim, who had returned to his driving task.

"Well, Marshal, it's good to see you again. And you've found the girl."

"And the heathen who killed Mr. Miller," Dan added.

Verity walked around to look into the wagon at Tom Blue, who was sitting sullenly in the corner.

"You'll be hanging him, then?"

"I can promise you that," Ned said.

"I never thought of myself as a bloodthirsty woman, Marshal. But I wish I could be there to see that."

"I'll send you the newspaper account," Ned said. "I'd appreciate that." Verity looked up at Laurel and smiled at her. "Listen to me, talking such a way when I'm trying to make a good impression on the girl here. Laurel, I'm not a mean-spirited woman, as you'll see if you'll come live with me."

Maybe it was the need, maybe it was the opportunity, but Laurel had never felt so warm, so quickly, toward another person. She smiled at Verity and, even as she did so, realized it was the first smile to cross her face in over a week.

"I think you have a fine spirit, Mrs. Miller," she said.

"Then you won't mind staying with me?"

71

"I'd love to stay with you."

Verity's eyes misted over, and she held out her arms. "Then, may I say welcome home, child? For from now on, and for as long as you want to call it so, this is your home."

Ned felt the hackles rise on the back of his neck. There was that woman's smile again. This time it was Laurel who made him think of Katy.

Chapter 10

"INDIAN, DID YOU KILL HER MAN?" Jim asked as they drove away.

"Yes," Tom Blue said.

"You got no feelin's about it one way or the other, do you?"

"I killed him for my friend."

"Luckless?"

"Yes."

"Good, good. When we catch that sonofabitch, we'll hang him for that. I've took a lot of folks back to Judge Barnstall for hangin', but I've never enjoyed a hangin' as much as I'm gonna enjoy watchin' you two."

"I will not hang," Tom Blue said as they left the Miller farm.

"Oh, yeah, you're gonna hang all right," Jim answered. "You're gonna hang, you sonofabitch, if I have to throw a rope over a tree and hang you myself."

"My warriors will not let me hang."

"Your warriors? You have no warriors, Indian. You have nothing but a band of cutthroats and cattle thieves. Only men of honor can lead warriors. You have no honor."

When they stopped to rest the horses awhile later, Jim passed on to Ned Tom Blue's confession to the murder of Clyde Miller and the fact that he had done it for Luckless. He also told Ned that Tom Blue believed he would be rescued.

"I'm like you. I don't want to dignify them by calling them warriors, but he's right when he says they'll try to break him loose."

"You got any idea where?" Jim asked.

Ned pointed to two buttes just ahead of them. "If they're going to hit us soon, I'd say that would be as good a place as any for it."

"You're probably right. All right, I'll keep my eyes open as we go through," Jim promised.

"And your weapons ready," Ned added.

As the marshals started between the buttes, all eyes were on the walls, the rocks, the enclaves, anywhere an ambusher might find some concealment. They rode into the little draw with hackles stiff as porcupine quills on the backs of their neck. Then, when they were fully committed, a rifle shot rang out, followed by the whine of a spent bullet. The Indians had not been hiding on the buttes, but nearby. When the marshals entered the pass, the Comanches rode into the canyon from the rear.

"There they are, behind us!" Ned shouted, and Jim Early rattled the reins, then used his whip on the team to get them out of the draw.

Ned, Dan, and Kurt fired back over their shoulders at the puff of smoke drifting away from the rifle shot. They weren't actually trying to hit anything, they wanted only to interfere with the brave who was shooting at them.

They rolled out of the other side of the small canyon formed by the twin buttes, the horses straining in the harness, the wheels throwing up rooster tails of dust. Arrows zipped by to stick in the ground in front of them, or to rattle off the nearby rocks. Bullets whined and hummed as they sizzled by, frying the air.

Half a dozen Comanches were giving chase and they broke out of the canyon after the wagon and outriders. The Comanches were painted for war and yelling at the top of their lungs as they fired their rifles and shot arrows toward the marshals. Ned realized he was out of range for accurate pistol shooting, so he slipped his handgun back into its holster, then pulled his rifle out of its scabbard. He twisted around in his saddle and held himself on by crooking his leg around the saddlehorn. He aimed as well as he could from the back of a galloping horse, but there was no way he could hold a target in his sights, so he had to snap shots off by guessing when he was lined up. The Henry bucked against his shoulder, and he was rewarded by the sight of one of the Indians grabbing his shoulder as blood spilled between the brave's fingers. Ned fired three more times before a second Comanche dropped his bow and grabbed a knee, shattered by Ned's bullet. Even with two wounded, however, the Comanches continued their pursuit for at least five more minutes before finally breaking off.

"They're leaving," Ned shouted. "Pull up. We'll give the horses a blow."

"Whoa, whoa there," Jim called, hauling back on the reins. The horses slowed, then came to a stop, the Black Maria sitting behind them wreathed in dust. The horses were breathing hard and their efforts had worked up a foam of sweat that slicked their hides. Ned, Dan, and Kurt brought their own animals to a halt, then dismounted to give them a rest as well.

"Anyone hurt?" Ned asked.

"I'm in one piece," Jim replied.

"I am not hurt," Dan added.

"Kurt? You all right?"

"*Ja*. I am fine," Kurt said. He looked back to see if any Comanches were coming after them. "Are they gone?"

"They'll be back," Ned said, taking a drink of water. He corked his canteen, then wiped the back of his hand across his mouth.

"I want water," Tom Blue said.

"Hand me the prisoner canteen," Ned said to Jim. He took the canteen and passed it through the bars to Tom Blue. He saw then that the prisoner was holding his hand to his nose. It was bleeding from the jouncing around of the wagon during the chase. "I guess it's pretty uncomfortable back there when the team is going all out," Ned said. "Hurt yourself?"

Tom Blue glared at him, but he said nothing. He took a drink, then handed the canteen back to Ned.

"Why don't you tell your friends to back off? You'd be a lot more comfortable." When there was still no response, Ned chuckled. "Well, I hope you enjoy the ride. Come on, men, let's get moving."

The horses rested, the party got under way again. Though no longer running the animals, they rode at a quick, ground-eating pace, always keeping their eyes open for another attack. There were no more mass attacks like the one between the buttes, but the Comanches did harass them along the trail, popping up at odd moments, shooting, making the trek a nightmare of nervous tension. Fear rode with them. It knotted up their bellies, swirled the bile in their guts and tautened the skin on their faces.

It was full dark by the time they reached Boiling Springs, where they stopped for the night. Ned decided there would be more security if two of them stayed awake at all times. He told Jim and Kurt to take the watch until midnight, while he and Dan would take over at midnight and go until dawn.

"Roll out," Jim whispered.

When Ned opened his eyes, Jim's hand was on his shoulder. He had slept so soundly that it seemed only a minute ago when he lay down.

"Anything happening?" he asked.

"Quiet as a church on Monday," Jim answered.

Ned took a drink of water from his canteen, then looked over to see Kurt and Dan exchanging places. He poured some water onto his hands and wet his eyes. It was at least five hours until dawn ... a long time to stay awake.

It was a little after four and Ned and Dan had been on guard for over four hours. Sleep pulled at Ned, and his eyes burned with tiredness. It had been an uneventful four hours, but within the last fifteen minutes there had been a change, a nuance so subtle that Ned was only barely aware.

"Dan?" Ned whispered.

"Yes?"

"Have you heard anything or seen anything?"

"No," Dan said. "But I have an itch."

"So do I."

Ned was glad to see that he wasn't alone with his nagging feeling. He sat on a nearby rock and looked out through the dark. One of the subtle things he had noticed was that the night had grown unnaturally quiet, as if even the small nocturnal animals and insects sensed hidden danger in the shadows.

Ned had no doubt that the Comanches were out there, close. He could practically smell their rankness in the air around him. Yet, as carefully as he scanned the dark, he could see no flicker of movement, hear no sound.

He got up to walk toward the jail wagon, intending to climb on top and use its height for a greater perspective of the land, when some sixth sense suddenly told him that they were dangerously near. He spun around, straining to see in the darkness, then saw several blobs of shadows moving through the darkness just a few feet away.

Ned drew and fired in one fluid motion. For an instant, the bright bloom from the muzzle blast painted the campsite in an eerie light. He saw four Indians nearly inside the camp. One of them fell wounded. The others returned his fire and another flash of light lit up the darkness. Ned heard the sound of an arrow thumping into flesh close by, and he knew one of his deputies was hit.

After that, there was no more sound except for the shuffle of feet hurrying through the brush as the Indians, their hope for surprise compromised, retreated. Ned looked out into the dark, but there was nothing to shoot at, only the quiet settling in once again. The Comanches had withdrawn, but he had no idea how far, or when they might return.

Both Jim and Kurt were up with guns in their hands, looking out into the darkness.

"Ned." Dan Norling's voice came to him, strained somewhat with pain. "Ned, I'm hit."

Ned holstered his pistol, then hurried to his friend. "How bad?"

"Maybe not so bad," Dan said. Ned was close to him now and saw the big Swede holding his shoulder. An arrow was sticking out of Dan's biceps, and a stream of blood spilled through his fingers and trickled down his arm.

"Damn," Jim drawled, holstering his own pistol. "Can't you fellas handle it when- it's your turn on watch? Did we wake you up for help when it was our turn?"

"Ja, we let you sleep in peace," Kurt added with a chuckle.

"I didn't ask you to help us. Did you ask for any help, Ned?" Dan asked.

"I didn't say a word. Far as I'm concerned you fellas could have slept right through the whole thing." Ned had been looking at the arrow wound the whole time he was talking. "Looks like it's lodged in some muscle. I'm going to pull it out."

"Yes, go ahead," Dan said.

Ned took a deep breath and put his hand on the shaft of the arrow. If the arrowhead was narrow it would come back out with little difficulty. If it was wide and flanged, it would tear flesh when he removed it. He jerked hard and the arrow came out fairly easily. It was a narrow point and little flesh was damaged.

"Could have been worse," Ned observed. He took the bottom of Dan's shirt out of his pants then tore off a long, wide, strip. He made a bandage of the strip and put it on Dan's wound.

"How is he?" Jim asked.

"He's all right," Ned said.

"Is that one dead?" Jim inquired, pointing to the Indian Ned had shot.

"He hasn't moved since I shot him, but it wouldn't hurt to check." Ned knew there was a chance that the Comanche might only be wounded. In that case, he might just lie there for the rest of the night, waiting for an opportunity to jump up and use his gun or a knife on one or more of them.

Jim walked over to the Indian and prodded the body with a rifle barrel, his finger ready on the trigger. When the Indian didn't react to his prodding, he bent down and touched the point of his knife against the Indian's flesh. He pushed the point in just enough to get a reaction from the Comanche if he was playing possum, but the Comanche didn't move. Jim knew then that he was dead. He stood up and put his knife back in his sheath.

"Well, there's one less Indian that'll be—" Jim's comment was cut off in mid-sentence by the whiz- whisper of a bullet, barreling into camp just ahead of the sound of a rifle shot. "Uhnnn," Jim said, and he dropped to one knee.

"Jim? Jim, what is it?" Ned asked.

Jim put his hand on his hip, then brought his fingers up and looked at them. Even in the imperfect light of the moon he could see the blood shining brightly.

"How do you like that?" Jim grunted. "One Indian out there in the dark somewhere takes a wild shot, and the bullet winds up here."

"You're hit?"

"Yeah."

"Where?"

"In the hip," he said. "I don't think it hit any of my vitals, but it's going to be a mite uncomfortable until we get back and I can get it out."

Ned had just finished bandaging Dan. Now he started on Jim, following the same procedure of using Jim's shirt.

"How is he?" Dan asked, coming over to stand by Jim as Ned worked on him. The red seepage through Dan's own bandage showed that the bleeding had not stopped.

"I'll be all right," Jim answered for himself. "Yeah, well, none of us are going to be all right if we don't do something, and do it damn soon."

"You got any ideas?" Jim asked.

"Maybe," Ned said. "But it's pretty desperate."

"Desperate, *ja,*" Kurt said, "but our situation is desperate. We must do what we must do."

"I'm glad you feel that way, pard, because I'm going to ask you to go off and leave us."

"Leave you? I don't understand."

"I've got an idea," Ned said.

"You don't sound like you like it much," said Jim sarcastically.

"I don't like it a damn bit," said Remington.

But he was thinking that it might save their lives . . . if it worked.

Chapter 11

"I DON'T KNOW," Jim said. "It galls me a little to put a cross over the grave of this heathen." Kurt hammered the cross into the ground at the head of the mound of dirt. Beneath the mound was the body of the Comanche Ned had killed.

"We want them to think it's one of us," Ned explained. "When they come after us, they are going to see what they believe is two prisoners in the back of the wagon with only one man, the driver, guarding them."

"And when they see Blue and me ride away, they'll think two of us have gone to look for help or more prisoners," Kurt said.

"Exactly."

"That's not gonna work, Ned, unless you put some white man's duds on Tom Blue."

"I'm glad you understand, Jim," Ned said with a smile.

"You're glad I understand? What do you mean?"

"You're the nearest his size."

"Oh no, not me. I'm not givin' up my other shirt and pants to that heathen."

"Don't worry about it."

"Don't worry about it? You want to wear the clothes after he had them on?"

"I'll ask Judge Barnstall if the court will buy you a new outfit when we get back," Ned promised.

"Yeah?" Jim walked over to his saddlebags and started pulling out another pair of pants and a shirt. "All right, but Tom Blue's gonna put on the clothes I'm wearin' now, with the bullet hole and blood on the pants and the torn shirt." He pulled off his shirt then started unbuttoning his pants. "I'm not givin' up a good set of duds to the sonofabitch."

"Dan, better get your shirt off, too," Ned said, taking his own off. "We have to look like Indians, remember?"

"How the hell you gonna do that? Your chest and back are white as a sheet."

"Here, let me do this," Kurt suggested. He began rubbing dirt onto Ned's back.

"Yeah, good idea," Ned agreed. He started rubbing dirt onto his arms and chest while Kurt was putting it on his back. Dan, as well as he could with the injured arm, began rubbing dirt onto himself, then he turned his back to Kurt to let the German finish the job.

"Put 'em on," Jim said, pointing out his discarded clothes to Tom Blue. When the Indian made no move toward them Jim pulled his pistol.

"I'd just as soon knock you out, Tom Blue, then dress you myself. I'm just givin' you a chance to save a knot on the head, that's all."

"This will not help," Tom Blue said, but because he realized that Jim would make good on his threat, he began putting on the clothes.

"We'll see," Ned said.

"Where do you want me to go with him?" Kurt asked, once Tom Blue was dressed.

"Handcuff him to the saddlehorn," Ned instructed. "Then swing on down toward El Reno."

"And what about the rest of you? Where are you going?"

"We'll keep on east until we reach Cleo Springs. There we'll go south along the Cimarron and rendezvous with you in Guthrie."

"If the heathens don't get us first," Jim said dryly.

"Ja, that is what I don't like about this," Kurt said. "You are going to be bait while I get away with the prisoner. You are calling all the danger to yourselves."

"That's exactly what I want to do. Dan and I will be in the back of the wagon, heavily armed. Since we buried the Comanche like he was one of us, the other Indians will think that one of theirs is still alive and our prisoner. When they see Dan and me in the wagon from a distance, they'll think it's Tom Blue and the Comanche they left behind. They won't want to shoot until they are sure they are close enough that they won't hit one of their own."

"What happens when they get that close?" Jim wanted to know.

"When they get that close, I don't want you to offer any resistance," Ned explained. "I want you to surrender, but be sure to keep your shotgun loaded and your pistols handy."

"You got it," Jim said, checking the load in his pistols.

"Well, let's get going. It'll be light soon. By the time the sun's full up I want to be on the trail."

Kurt and his prisoner had been on the trail for the better part of three hours. It was mid-morning and the day's heat was already oppressive. He shoved his hat back and mopped at his face with his bandana. He glanced over at Tom Blue and saw with a faint irritability that the Indian didn't appear to be feeling the heat like he was.

A dry, rattling wind lifted dust from the plains. The dust cloud swirled high on the hot, rising air and spread a red halo around the sun. Even the sky lost its blue, to be replaced by a dingy orange color.

Though some farmers were trying to make a go here, Kurt knew that the soil was thin and poor. It was short grass country, better for cattle than for crops. Plow its slopes up and down, or in contours, it would make no difference. The wind would lift the topsoil off, or flash floods would pour across the land in any direction, laying fields bare and cutting new gullies through them.

Even cattlemen were having a rough time of it, Kurt knew. They faced destructive tornadoes in the spring, blistering heat and terrible drought in the summer. It was even worse in the winter when a blue norther, as the storms were called, would set cattle helplessly drifting to huddle, frozen and starved, in fields of white.

Despite all that, there was a steady and ever increasing encroachment of white settlers into what had been designated as Indian Territory. With the wagon trains, cattle trails, railroads, and towns, this area would soon be as populated as the rest of the country. Until that time, the whole territory would depend upon the deputies of Judge Barnstall's court to administer the law, keep the peace. It was an obligation that Kurt, who had a profound respect for the law, appreciated.

Ahead there was a steep, sandstone rim. Kurt got off to lead his horse. He thought about letting Tom Blue dismount as well, but decided to keep him in the saddle. The Indian could handle it. If not, if he fell out of his saddle, well, that would be just too bad.

They made it down the rim all right, and Kurt swung into his saddle again. Ahead of them Kurt could see a forest of cedars and pine. The forest promised some cool respite from the sun, and he looked forward to reaching it.

They came to a creek with a stream of water perhaps two feet wide. The water glistened in the sun and looked cool and sweet.

"Want some water?" Kurt offered.

"Yes."

Kurt filled his tin cup, then held it to the Indian's lips. After the Indian had his fill, Kurt drank. He thought of a cold beer and wished he could have one now. He thought of Ned and Dan and Jim, and he wondered how they were getting along . . . whether the Indians had jumped them yet.

"I don't know what kind of view you fellas got from back there," Jim said under his breath, "but we got company."

"Where?" Ned asked.

"Off to the left about two hundred yards. They been ridin' just on the other side of the ridgeline there."

Ned was sitting with his legs drawn up in front of him. Without being too obvious, he looked over toward the ridgeline and saw the riders moving quickly, silently, expertly, with the wagon.

"I see them," Ned said. "You have the Greener ready?"

"Both barrels loaded with double-ought buck," Jim answered.

"Dan?"

"Both barrels, double-ought shot," Dan said.

Ned reached down to touch his own shotgun. Among the three of them they had six ten-gauge, double-ought charges ready. At close range it was enough firepower to stop a small army. But it all depended on getting the Indians up close, and that was the crux of Ned's plan.

"When they get close enough that they know you've seen them, stop and throw up your hands," Ned explained, "I want them to come all the way down here. Dan and I will be ready for them. When you hear us shoot, open up with everything you've got."

"All right, I'm ready for 'em," Jim said.

It was at least five more minutes until the wagon reached a ford known as Cimarron Crossing. There the Indians broke into the clear, obviously intending to attack as soon as the wagon was in midstream. Jim surprised them by pulling to a stop before they even reached him. He threw up his hands.

There were at least nine in the party of Indians that rode toward the wagon, and two more who stayed behind. The two who stayed behind were out of shotgun range and would probably get away, but if the others kept coming, they were doing exactly what Ned wanted them to do.

"You can have them," Jim called to the Indians as they came up. "I don't want any trouble."

"White man is a coward," one of the Indians said. "Look how easy he gives up."

"I just don't want no trouble, is all," Jim said, playing the game with them. He pointed to his hip. "I done been shot once, I don't want to get shot again." He pulled up his shirt. "Look at this."

What he was actually trying to do was keep the Indians' attention diverted away from the back of the wagon. He watched them, his right hand sneaking down to the seat to grasp his shotgun, while the Indians gathered at the rear of the wagon. One of their number broke the lock. Ned and Dan were sitting up front with their legs still drawn up, their faces on their knees. The door swung open and one of the Comanches grunted something, probably an invitation to get out.

"Now!" Ned shouted. His left hand had been on the Greener ten gauge. He lifted it up from the floor, letting off a blast as it came up. The face of the Indian who had broken the lock turned to pulp as the charge of shot hit him full force. Dan's gun discharged a second after that and another Indian went down, while Jim was close behind, dropping a third.

The Indians were caught completely off guard. One of them tried to fit an arrow into his bow, but the second shot from Ned's gun swept him off his horse. All three white men were firing at point-blank range, and Comanches began falling like rain. It was over in less than thirty seconds. Nine Comanches lay dead or dying in the dirt while Ned, Dan, and Jim were unscratched.

The two Indians who had stayed back looked on in shock. One of them raised his rifle and took a shot toward the wagon, but when the driver picked up a rifle and returned fire, the Indian heard a bullet whistle just inches away from his head. He turned and rode away at a frantic gallop with his companion right behind him.

The one who had taken a shot toward the wagon was called Billy Blackhat. The other was Rufus Coyote. Billy Blackhat and Rufus Coyote were the first to join Tom Blue, and they felt a special obligation in getting him free. They- knew now that they had been tricked, and their blood ran hot.

"Before, I wanted only to free Tom Blue," Billy said. "Now I want more. I want to kill the big white man who leads the others."

"We will," Rufus promised. "But not just the big man who leads them. We will kill them all."

Seething with rage, the two Comanches rode hard, not to get away from the marshals, but to vent their anger. They rode hard for an hour before they saw three white men ahead of them.

"They are there!" Billy shouted, pulling his rifle. "How did they get there?"

"No! It is not the marshals. It is the trader, Luckless. The two men with him are Moorhead and Butler, the ones who gave us whiskey to use the girl."

Billy sheathed his rifle and they rode on to meet the white men.

After hearing the story of the fight from Rufus Coyote, Nate Luckless gave the Indians a little whiskey to calm them down. Then, as they were passing the bottle back and forth, he nodded to Frank Moorhead and Willis Butler, indicating that he wanted to talk to them.

86

"I should'a knowed better'n to let a bunch of Indians take care of it," Nate said. "If ye' want somethin' done, it's better to do it yerself."

"What are you talkin' about?" Frank asked.

"The marshals," Nate said. "We're goin' to have to kill them, ye' know. We're gonna have to kill ever' one of 'em. 'Cause iffen we don't they'll be comin' after us next."

"You say that liken we could just go out an' do it. Seems to me like they're gonna take a lot of killin'," Willis suggested.

"No more'n anybody else," Nate insisted.

"I reckon that's what the Comanches thought. They've been doggin' them all this time, an' so far they ain't none of the marshals dead, but they have kilt ten of the ones that's followin' them."

"That don't mean nothin'," Nate said. "The Indians was suckered in, that's all. Ye' know Indians, they ain't very smart. With a little thinkin' we can handle it easy."

"I don't care how smart you be, they's still four of them an' only three of us. I don't like them kind of odds."

"Five of us," Nate said. "Don't forget them two. We'll let Billy Blackhat and Rufus Coyote join up with us. That way it'll be five of us with some smarts against the four of them ... and them tied down with tryin' to get Tom Blue back to Missouri."

"We gonna try an' rescue Tom Blue?" Frank asked. Nate looked over at Billy and Rufus. He hadn't given them enough whiskey to get drunk, and they were just finishing it. He spoke low so they couldn't overhear him.

"That's what I told them. And, if we can get him out we will, but we ain't gonna bust no gut tryin'. The main thing is to stop the marshals from gettin' back. If it comes down to it an' the only way we can do it is to kill Blue in the bargain, then I don't intend to let that stop me."

"I reckon keepin' the marshals from gettin' back is the main thing for you," Frank said. "They gonna try'n shut down your tradin' post. But they ain't got nothin' agin' Willis an' me, an' I don't see why we ought to take the chance."

"Oh, they don't have nothin' agin' ye', eh? Ye' think maybe that girl you raped didn' say nothin' a'tall about who done it?" Luckless challenged.

"He's right, Frank," Willis said, speaking for the first time. "Iffen that girl told the marshals about us, they're gonna be comin' for us, too. An' they'll be hangin' us for it more'n likely."

Luckless smiled, an evil smile. "Now, do we follow the wagon tracks or not?"

"I reckon we got no choice," Frank agreed.

Chapter 12

IT WAS LATE AFTERNOON and the sun was a brilliant red orb, four fingers above the western horizon, when Kurt saw Guthrie rising into view on the plains before him. A shimmer of sunlight bounced off the shingled roofs and clapboard sidings of the dozen or so buildings that made up the town. Prodding his horse, he and his prisoner rode down the nearly deserted street past a few staked-out lots . . . signs of the town's ambition.

A kiosk in the middle of the street advertised "Bitter Ash," and around the kiosk two little boys were playing a game of tag. The McKenzie Mercantile Store stood right across from the kiosk. McKenzie Mercantile was twice as wide and twice as high as any other store in town, and nearly equaled the hotel in size. The lone, many claimed, was the most elegant hotel in the territory, if one discounted some of the really fine hotels already established in the Nations.

Kurt and his prisoner rode on through the town until he could see the jailhouse at the far end of the street. Right next door to the jailhouse was the Stockwell Saloon, and Kurt could already taste the beer he would be drinking in a few minutes. The large sign touting the saloon hung out over the boardwalk, squeaking an invitation as it rocked in the evening breeze.

Kurt rode straight to the jail, then dismounted and tied both horses to the rail.

"Do you think you can keep me here?" Tom Blue asked.

"Do you think not?"

"I think no," Blue replied. "I will not hang."

"Ja, you will hang, Tom Blue," Kurt promised. "Maybe you will already be dead when the rope is put around your neck, but I promise you, you will hang." Kurt unlocked the Indian from his saddlehorn, then pulled him down and locked the handcuffs again.

"Now, get in there," he said, shoving the Indian in front of him.

Inside the sheriff's office, a big-boned young man, perhaps twenty-five or so, sat behind a desk, busily polishing a lamp chimney. He was wearing a five-pointed deputy sheriff's badge, and when Kurt pushed his prisoner in ahead of him, the deputy stood up.

"What's going on here? Who are you? What are you bringing him in here for?" he asked.

"This is my prisoner, wanted on a federal warrant from Judge Barnstall's court in Stone County, Missouri. I want you to put him up for me."

The man shook his head. "I'm just the deputy here, I got no authority to put anyone in jail."

"I'm a U.S. Deputy Marshal," Kurt said. "I have all the authority that is needed."

"I don't know about that," the town deputy hedged. "You can't come in here and. just take over."

Kurt glared at the young deputy. "I have been in the Nations and the territory for more than two weeks," he said. "I have been rained on, shot at, gone without food and drink. Now I am in a town, and I am going to put this man in your jail," Kurt said resolutely. "You can either guard him or join him', it makes no difference to me."

The deputy hurried over to the wall and took down a large ring of keys.

"I'll put him in, mister," he grumbled. "But you're gonna have to talk to Sheriff Epperson about keepin' him in here."

"I'll be glad to talk to your sheriff. Where can I find him?"

"Next door, in the Stockwell Saloon."

Kurt smiled. "In the saloon, you say? Tell me, is their beer cold?"

"It should be. I was down to the icehouse yesterday and there was plenty of ice left," the deputy said.

"Ah, good, good. That was going to be my first stop. It will be a pleasure to talk to your sheriff."

"Come on, you," the deputy said, pushing an unresisting Tom Blue into the cell. He closed and locked the door, then looked back at Kurt. "You say you're a federal deputy?"

"Yes."

"What'd this here Indian do? Get drunk on the reservation?"

"*Ja,* I'm sure he did that," Kurt said.

"And you're takin' him all the way back to Missouri for that?"

"For that, and for other things."

"What other things?"

"I'm sure we'll find plenty to charge him with."

"What's his name, anyway?" the deputy asked curiously. He was standing right at the door looking into Tom Blue's face.

"Tom Blue," Kurt said.

"Tom Blue?" The deputy gasped, then realized he was standing very close to the cell door, too close for him to be comfortable. He stepped away quickly, so quickly it was almost a jump.

"Uh, look," the deputy said. "You ain't gonna leave me alone with him, are you? I've heard about this redskin. He's one mean sonofabitch."

"He is handcuffed and he is locked in his cell," Kurt said. "What can he do?"

"Just don't leave me alone with him," the deputy said, backing still farther away from the cell door.

"You'll be all right," Kurt said as he left the jail. "I'll tell the sheriff you have company."

As soon as Kurt left the jail, the deputy returned to the desk. He opened the drawer, pulled out a pistol, and sat there holding it as he looked over at the Indian in the cell. He turned the cylinders to check the load, then looked up at the prisoner again. After a moment, he decided the pistol wasn't enough so he went to the gun rack and pulled down a Greener, ten-gauge, double barrel. He broke open the barrels and slid in two double-ought shells, snapped the barrels closed, then looked toward the cell again. He held the Greener in his lap and put the pistol on the comer of the desk.

"Don't get any ideas, Tom Blue," he said. "'Cause you ain't goin' nowhere while Angus Conn is on the job."

Tom Blue glanced at the nervous deputy, snorted once, then lay down on the bunk.

There was only one saloon in town. It was called the Stockwell Saloon, and right under the swinging sign which hung over the sidewalk, there was another sign alongside the door. This was a big picture of a beer mug, golden yellow at the bottom, white foam at the top. The price, 5C, was nearly as large as the beer mug. Kurt licked his dry lips as he saw it, then stepped inside.

The one thing Kurt missed about working in the Nations was that it was absolutely dry. Only when you left the Nations to come over into the Oklahoma territory could you expect to find liquor, and not always then. You could always count on Guthrie, though. Some said it would be the capital if this territory ever became a state.

There were half a dozen men and one woman inside the saloon. There were four, who appeared to be cowhands, sitting together at one of the tables. One customer, thick-bodied, bearded, and gray, stood at the bar, staring sourly at the mug of beer in front of him. The sixth person was the bartender, tall and gaunt with a coal-black spade beard and a neatly trimmed mustache.

The woman was sitting in a chair by the wall where a piano would be, if there had been a piano. Like so many establishments in the territory, the Stockwell didn't want to go to the expense of having one shipped out, then bear the additional expense of paying someone to play it.

The woman, seeing someone new come into the bar, smiled broadly and walked over to meet him. Kurt guessed that she was in her early thirties, though her face was older and her eyes ancient.

"You're new in town aren't you, mister?" the woman said.

"Just passing through," Kurt answered. "I'm looking for your sheriff."

The thick-bodied gent took a long drink of his beer, wiped the foam off his beard with the back of his hand, then turned toward Kurt.

"What do you want with him?"

"Are you the sheriff?"

"Matter of fact, I am."

"I just put a prisoner in your jail."

"You put a prisoner in my jail? What the hell for?"

"Because I do not want him to get away," Kurt explained. He turned so the sheriff could see his badge. "I'm a U.S. Deputy Marshal."

"Deputies don't mean shit to me, mister," the sheriff said. "Even a federal deputy."

"The U.S. Marshal I ride for will be in tomorrow," Kurt said. "Do you feel the same way about all U.S. Marshals?"

"Who is this marshal you ride for?"

"Remington. Ned Remington."

The sheriff's eyes narrowed, then he grunted.

"I know Remington," he said. "Whyn't you tell me who it was? If Remington wants to bed a man down in my jail, I'll be glad to do it."

"Thanks," Kurt said.

"Who you got?"

"Tom Blue."

"Tom Blue? A Comanche, with a scar on his face?"

"Ja. That is him."

Sheriff Epperson let out a low whistle. "He's a mean one," he said. "I think maybe I ought to send somebody over to stay with Conn."

"Conn. That your deputy?"

"Yes."

Kurt smiled. "I think he will appreciate having someone with him."

"I'll keep the guard doubled all night. I'm real glad to see that redskin got hisself caught, an' I wouldn't want to see him get away."

Sheriff Epperson left the saloon and walked across the street to the Hotel Ione. Guthrie had no mayor or city council, but it did have an unofficial town board. Epperson knew that most of them would be in the hotel lobby playing cards. Otis Mayfield, the hotel owner, was president of the town board.

The game was in full progress. There were five men engaged, with a pile of chips in the middle of, and a cloud of cigar smoke spread just over, the table. Mayfield, a hatchet-faced, raw-boned man, looked up when Sheriff Epperson entered. He had just shoved in a chip as the ante was raised.

"Well, I know you didn't come to join our game, Sheriff," he said. "So what is it? Some drunks acting up again?"

"No," Epperson said. "I need three dollars from the town board."

"Three dollars? What for?"

"I'm puttin' on two extra guards at the jail tonight. I'll be needin' to pay them."

"Three aces, gentlemen. Read 'em an' weep," Mayfield said, turning up his cards to display the winning hand. With groans and sighs of disgust, the remaining players threw in their hands, and Mayfield raked in the winnings.

"Tell me, Sheriff, why is it necessary to put on extra guards tonight?" Loomis McKenzie asked. McKenzie owned the mercantile store that dominated the town.

"We've got a special prisoner in tonight," Epperson said. "Tom Blue."

Mayfield, who was gathering the cards to shuffle, stopped and looked up at Epperson.

"Tom Blue? Look here, you mean the Comanche renegade?"

"Yes," Epperson said.

McKenzie slammed his hand on the table. "Damnation, Epperson! What the hell did you have to go and arrest that Indian for? What are you trying to do? Be a hero? Get a name for yourself? Hold us up for more money?"

Epperson looked at McKenzie, surprised by his outbreak.

"I don't understand," he said. "You act like you'd rather not see him in jail."

"You're damn right I'd rather not see him in jail," McKenzie said. "Maybe in somebody else's jail, but not in *our* jail. I've got too much to lose in this town. You want the entire Comanche nation down on our backs, killing our people, burning our stores?"

"Which are you most worried about, Mr. McKenzie?" Epperson asked coldly. "Killing our people or burning our stores?"

"You know what I mean," Epperson sputtered. "I'm not sure that I do. Anyway, I didn't arrest Tom Blue. He was brought in by a United States Deputy Marshal. I wish I had arrested the Indian. Besides, he's a renegade. The good Comanches probably want him out of the way as much as we do. They aren't going to come down on us."

"If not the Comanches, then some of their renegade friends," McKenzie said. "What difference does it make whether our stores are burned by good Comanches or renegades? They'll bum just as well."

"Well, tell me, Mr. McKenzie, what do you propose I do?" Epperson asked, growing a little disgusted with McKenzie's attitude.

"Let him go," McKenzie said.

"What? Are you crazy? I couldn't do that, even if I wanted to. I told you, he isn't my prisoner, he was brought in by a U.S. Deputy Marshal."

"Then tell the U.S. Deputy Marshal that the Indian is his responsibility. If he wants to keep him, take him somewhere else, somewhere outside of town, and keep him there."

"You can't be serious," Epperson said.

"Now, wait a minute. Loomis has a point, John," Mayfield suggested. "After all, we're down here pretty much on our own. We don't have any state law, or even territorial law to protect us. All we have is the federal law, and it's too far away to do us any good. No, sir, the best way to handle this matter is just to stay out of it."

"We can't stay out of it," Sheriff Epperson said. "He's in our jail and he's going to stay there until the marshal moves on with him."

Mayfield shuffled the cards then as if dismissing Epperson.

"All right, Sheriff, let him stay in your jail. But don't expect the town board to come up with three dollars extra to take care of someone else's prisoner. We got to raise that money from licenses and taxes, and it isn't fair to our citizens to expect them to bear the cost of a federal prisoner. Gentlemen, I open for three dollars," he said, sliding the chips into the center. The others answered his opening bet. Mayfield looked up at Epperson. "Is there anything else?" he asked.

"No," Epperson said through teeth clenched in anger, "there is nothing else."

Chapter 13

"I'M SORRY," Sheriff Epperson said to Kurt when he returned to the saloon to talk to him. ''The town board turned me down when I asked for money to hire extra guards. You can keep him in my jail, but you're going to have to keep an eye on him yourself."

Kurt sighed. ''All right," he said. ''I didn't really want a bath and a room. It would make me feel guilty that my friends are still out on the prairie while I was fresh and clean, sleeping between sheets."

Sheriff Epperson laughed. "Yes, I'm sure it would. Well, I can't promise you a bath or clean sheets, Deputy, but there is an empty cell next to your prisoner, and it's got a cot you can use."

"What about your deputy?"

"Angus Conn? He's a pretty good man ... a little young and inexperienced, maybe. I think he has more gumption than anyone gives him credit for, including himself. At least he doesn't bore you with boisterous talk like so many his age. He's just an all-around dependable man who does what he has to, and I don't think you can ask for much more than that. Anyway, he'll stay with you until ten. I'll be making my rounds until midnight, then I'll turn in for the night myself. Before I do, though, I'll stop by to see if you need anything."

''I appreciate this, Sheriff," Kurt said. "Do you have any objections to my buying you a beer?"

"None at all," the sheriff said, signaling to the bartender.

It was just before eleven o'clock, and Kurt was sure Angus Conn was asleep by now, probably in a bed with real sheets. He envied the deputy.

Kurt was lying on the ticking mattress of the cell cot, looking at the slow, steady breathing of Tom Blue in the cell next to him. It was hot, so hot that for a moment Kurt felt as if he couldn't get his breath. Finally, with a sigh, he went outside onto the porch for some cool, fresh air. That was when two people ran by in front of him. One of them went on to the saloon to yell at the patrons inside while the other stopped in front of Kurt.

"You the U.S. Deputy Marshal I heard about?" he asked excitedly.

"Yes."

"Maybe you better get down to the livery, right away," he said.

"Why? What is it? What's going on?"

"The sheriff was a fool to go down there by his- self."

"What happened?"

"There was a couple of cowboys got liquored up in the saloon, started causin' trouble," the man explained. "The sheriff run 'em out of the saloon, told 'em to go on out to the ranch and sober up. But they only got as far as the livery then one of 'em kilt the stable boy. The livery owner got away and come for the sheriff, but the two cowboys say they're gonna kill him iffen he comes for 'em."

Kurt looked back inside the jail. Was this some sort of trick, some setup by Tom Blue's friends? If he went down to help the sheriff, would they come in the back way and take Tom Blue out of jail?

He knew that was a very strong possibility, but he also knew that the problem the sheriff was facing might have nothing at all to do with his prisoner. It might be just what it appeared to be, and if it was, he couldn't leave a fellow law officer, even a local badge totter, to go it alone. Sheriff Epperson was helping him by keeping Tom Blue in jail against the wishes of the town board. Now it was only right that he help Sheriff Epperson.

"I'll go down there," Kurt offered.

"Good," the man said, genuinely pleased. "I'll go an' wake up Angus."

Kurt started toward the livery and was almost there when he heard a muffled gunshot from the dark. He started toward the livery on the run, then he saw Sheriff Epperson coming out of the shadows toward him.

"Sheriff? Sheriff, what is it? What's going on?" Kurt called. "I heard a shot."

Kurt saw a peculiar glowing, then he realized that it was a circle of fire. Epperson's coat was burning!

"I'm killed, Deputy," the sheriff said with a half smile on his face. He fell face down to the ground and Kurt ran over to him. He rolled the sheriff over and patted out the ring of fire on his jacket. That was when he realized what had caused the fire in the first place.

Sheriff Epperson had been shot at point-blank range, 'and the powder blast from the revolver had set his jacket ablaze. That was also why the gunshot had sounded muffled.

"There goes one of 'em, Deputy!" a man shouted from the other side of the livery. Kurt drew his pistol and stared into the inky darkness.

A figure suddenly appeared near the corner of the livery barn. He was tall and lanky with a bushy, walrus-type mustache. He wore a high-crowned hat of the type favored by the range cowboys, and Kurt saw a flash of light from one of the rowels on his spurs. The man pointed his pistoL toward Kurt, and it boomed three times. In the light of the muzzle-flash, Kurt could see the almost demonic features of his face.

Kurt shot back, only once, but once was enough. His bullet found its mark, for the man suddenly threw up his gun then fell over backward. Kurt ran over to him and knelt beside him. He could see bubbles of blood oozing from the man's mouth. The wounded stranger was trying hard to breathe, and Kurt heard a sucking sound in the man's chest. He knew then that his bullet, had punctured the gunman's lungs.

"Is the sonofabitch dead?" a new voice asked calmly from behind the German's back. Kurt looked around to see the first of the townspeople approaching. Beyond him, a large crowd surged forward in the darkness.

"Who are you?" Kurt asked.

"I'm Loomis McKenzie. I own the McKenzie Mercantile Store."

Kurt dropped his pistol in his holster and looked down at the man he had just shot.

"He will be shortly," he said. "Dead, I mean." McKenzie looked down at the mortally wounded gunman. "That there's Grady Martin," McKenzie said. "He's always been a hell-raiser . . . never thought he'd shoot anyone."

"It....it wam't s'posed to go like this," Grady said. He wheezed and tried to cough out the gob of blood that choked his throat. "Me'n Poke was just s'pose to make a little noise. Nobody know'd the

stable boy would come at us with a pitchfork like he done. I didn't have no choice. I had to shoot him. Then, when the sheriff come after us, Poke hid behind the door. The sheriff come right in, just liken as if he'd been invited. Poke stuck the barrel into the sheriff's belly and pulled the trigger. That was two folks kilt an' all we was s'posed to do was make a little noise."

"What? What do you mean make a little noise?" Kurt asked.

"You know, shoot up the town a little, get you an' the sheriff away from the jail."

"My prisoner!" Kurt said. "My God, they're after my prisoner!"

He leaped up and ran back down the street to the jail. When he got inside, he saw a face at the window at the rear of Tom Blue's cell. He snapped off a quick shot and, though he missed, the face disappeared. Kurt ran through the jail, then dashed out the back door, where he saw a shadow slip just around the comer at the far end of the alley. He fired a second time and saw a spray of splinters where his bullet hit the comer of the building right behind the intruder. But again, he missed. He ran down to the end of the alley and saw two riders galloping away on horseback.

When he returned to the sheriff's office, McKenzie, Angus Conn, and one other man were there waiting for him. Conn looked sad. McKenzie introduced the other man as Mayfield, president of the town board. Both McKenzie and Mayfield seemed very angry.

"Did the cowhand die?" Kurt asked.

Conn nodded.

"The other name he mentioned, Poke. Anybody know anything about him?"

"That would be Poke Patterson," Conn contributed. "Him an' Grady ran together all the time. Never seen one of 'em, without seein' the other one."

"What about it? Where is he now?"

"Somebody said they seen 'im ridin' off to the northwest," Conn said.

"I want you to know that I hold you personally responsible for this, Deputy," McKenzie said.

"You mean killing the cowpoke? Yeah, sure, I'm responsible. But he fired at me first. I had no choice."

"You had a choice when you brought that renegade into our jail.

"Tom Blue. Yeah. So?"

"He's the cause of it all," Mayfield said.

"Yes," McKenzie added. "Before Grady died, he said a big, bald-headed, bearded man hired him an' Poke to do this," McKenzie said. "You know anybody who fits that description?"

"That would be Nate Luckless. We have a warrant for him, too."

"He a friend of this man you've got in jail?"

"You might say that," Kurt said dryly.

"This whole thing was just so's they could come in and steal your prisoner, wasn't it?"

"It was so they could try," Kurt admitted. "As a matter of fact, they did try, but they didn't get the job done."

"No, but they come close enough that three of our citizens was kilt here tonight."

"Three?" Kurt asked in surprise.

"Yes. The stable boy, Sheriff Epperson, and Grady Martin."

Kurt snorted. "Grady Martin brought this on himself. I wouldn't count him as one of your first-class citizens."

"What about the stable boy and the sheriff? They are both dead."

"I'm sorry about that. The sheriff was a good man," Kurt said.

"I told the sheriff this would happen," McKenzie said. "When he came to the board for more money, I told him he was opening the town to danger just by taking your prisoner. I tried to get him to turn you out, and he wouldn't do it. I reckon this just proves my point."

"What are trying to say, Mr. McKenzie?" Kurt asked tiredly.

"I think," McKenzie started, then he cleared his throat and, with a wave of his hand, took in Mayfield as well. "That is we think—and we are speaking for the town board here—that you should take your prisoner out of town. Keep him out on the prairie overnight. Sheriff Epperson said you were waiting for Marshal Remington to show up. When he shows up you can move on.

"We tried to get Epperson to tell you that, but he wouldn't do it. Well, he's gone now so there's nothing to keep us from running you out."

"We ain't gonna do that, Mr. Mayfield," Conn said quickly.

Mayfield and McKenzie looked over at the young deputy as if shocked at what they heard.

"What'd you say?"

Conn cleared his throat. "I said we ain't gonna make Deputy Hammer take his prisoner outta town to wait. Sheriff Epperson told him he could keep his prisoner here, an' that's the way it's gonna be."

"You're just the deputy sheriff," Mayfield sputtered. "Who the hell are you to tell us what to do?"

"I *was* the deputy sheriff," Conn said. "But now that Sheriff Epperson's dead, I'm the acting sheriff. Leastwise until you can call a town board meetin' to get someone else swore in. And I don't think you want to do that just yet."

"Careful, Angus Conn. You're getting a little too big for your britches," Mayfield warned.

"Maybe," Conn said. He hitched up his trousers. "Or maybe I'm just now fillin' them."

McKenzie and Mayfield fumed at their deputy, but Kurt walked over and stood beside him, face to face with the two town businessmen, challenging them to go further.

"Gentlemen, if that will be all, I'd suggest you leave the jailhouse now. I drove one man away from the window. Who knows who might be lurking out there in the dark now, just waiting for another shot? If they start shooting while you two are in here, one of you might get hurt."

The two men looked startled at that idea. Realizing the validity of it, they quickly turned on their heels and hurried away. On the way out they promised to "have this all out the next day."

Conn walked over to the door and watched them until they were a full block away, then he closed the door and walked back to sit behind the desk. The two lanterns he had cleaned earlier in the day were both lit and glowing brightly.

"I reckon we can count on Poke joining up with the fellas that's comin' after this Indian," Conn said. "He sure skedaddled outta here."

"What's Poke look like?"

"He's about five foot nine or ten," Conn said. "Got a narrow face, beady eyes, kind of a scraggly black beard. He's sure not what the womenfolk would call a good-lookin' critter."

Kurt chuckled. "Good enough description, I'll know him if I ever see him." He walked over and turned the wick down on one of the lanterns. The flame sputtered and died. A plume of smoke rose from the darkened glass chimney. "I guess if I'm going to stay here tonight, it would make less of a target if I killed some of the light."

"Good idea," Conn replied. He looked around. "Where do you want me? Up front or in the back?"

"You're staying? I thought you were off for the night."

"That's when I was the deputy. Now that I'm the sheriff I reckon I better start acting like one.

Kurt smiled. "Angus, in my book it isn't acting," he said. "You are the sheriff."

About five miles out of town, underneath a canopy of cottonwood leaves, Nate Luckless, Frank Moorhead, Willis Butler, along with Billy Blackhat, were listening to Poke Patterson tell what happened in the town.

"Me an' Grady started raisin' hell in the saloon, just like you told us to," Poke told them, "an' the sheriff run us out of the saloon, just like we thought he would. After that, me an' Grady went down to the livery stable. We was just goin' to shoot up the place a little, but this here stable boy come at us with a pitchfork. Grady kilt the stable boy, an' when the sheriff come in after us, I kilt him."

"I wanted you to get the U.S. Deputy Marshal to come down there," Luckless said.

"Hell, he did come down. He come down there long enough to kill Grady," Poke protested.

"Yes, but not long enough for us to do our job," Luckless said. "We got to the jail and got a look-see, but the marshal got back too quick."

"What are we goin' to do now, Nate?" Butler asked.

Nate tugged on his beard. "Well, we got Rufus Coyote trailin' the wagon. It'll probably get here before light in the mornin'. I'll come up with somethin' else."

"Whatever you come up with, count me in," Poke said. "Grady was my friend. I want revenge."

"We can always use an extra gun," Nate assured him.

But he trusted the wastrel like he trusted the Comanche.

Not a damn bit.

Chapter 14

JAMES RANSOM EARLY shifted his weight on the seat, but it didn't help. The pain in his hip washed over him in waves, and his leg throbbed with a fever like the heat from hornet stings. He knew the bullet was going to have to come out, or the wound would mortify on him. If it mortified, it wouldn't do any good to cut off his leg to stop the poison because the wound was too high up for that. If it mortified, Jim would die.

Dan moved up front to sit on the seat beside Jim. "Let me take the team," he said.

"Dan, thanks," said Early, gritting his teeth against the pain.

Ned, who had given his horse to Kurt for Tom Blue, was riding Dan's horse alongside the wagon.

"How are you doing?" Ned asked. "You want to stop for the night?"

"No," Jim answered. "Unless you are planning to dig this bullet out of me."

"I'd rather not try and take it out unless I have to," Ned said. "Doc Urban lives in Guthrie."

"You know him? He ever take out a bullet before?" Ned chuckled. "He was a Confederate surgeon

during the war, and I reckon he took out enough bullets to fight a battle. Don't worry, you'll be in good hands once we get you there."

"Then let's keep goin'." Jim grimaced. "How much farther is it, anyway?"

"At this rate, I make it about five more hours," Ned answered. "If we keep going all night, we'll be there before light. Can you hold on that long?"

"I got no choice," Jim said. "I'll hold on."

"How about you, Dan? How's your shoulder coming along?"

"A little sore is all," Dan answered, putting his hand over the wound. "The arrow is out so my wound can heal. It is not like Jim, where every shake and bump of the wagon moves the bullet."

"Hang on, Jim," Ned encouraged.

"Yeah, well, I'm going to do my damnedest," Jim answered dryly.

Ned rode on ahead of the wagon, scouting the road to make certain they didn't run into any bad holes or oversized bumps.

Ned knew what it felt like to have a bullet lodged inside your body, heavy and burning, pressing against the nerves and arteries so that every bump made it feel as if the bullet were tearing into the flesh anew. Ned's own body was a crazy quilt of scars from knife wounds and bullet holes, going all the way back to his very first wound, suffered at the Battle of Shiloh.

Ned had been hit by shell shrapnel on the evening of the first day of that bloody battle. Because of the ebb and flow of the fighting that day, there were dead and wounded scattered over an area of ten square miles, and Confederate and Yankee soldiers were lying within half a dozen feet of each other. The first day's fighting had left a total of nearly ten thousand casualties, counting the dead and wounded of both sides, and as night fell the sound of their groans and moans were piteous to even the most hardened ears.

It had been dark and overcast on that first night, without moon or stars to light the way, so good Samaritans from both sides carried bobbing lanterns through the battlefield, helping when they could, giving water and comfort when they found someone beyond help. Often Confederate wounded were tended by Yankee corpsmen, Yankees wounded by Confederate medical-aid men. Sometimes there was cooperation between pairs of medical men on both sides as they pointed out locations to each other, or even helped when they could.

The man who had come to tend to Ned on that night was wearing the uniform of his enemy, but the help was not withheld. The man in the enemy uniform, the one who came to Ned's side, was James Ransom Early.

Ned looked over at Jim and saw that his friend's eyes were closed. Whether he was asleep or passed out, Ned didn't know. He knew only that either way it would be easier on Jim than if he had to face it totally conscious.

For Jim, the terrible pain had stopped and a warming numbness set in. It was that numbness which allowed Jim to endure the jouncing of the wagon. But with the deadening of pain came also a weakness from loss of blood, and by the time they rolled into Guthrie, Jim was staying conscious only by a supreme effort of will.

"Ned, I think Jim is about to keel over," Jim heard Dan call. He wanted to speak up, to tell them that he was all right, but he found that he was too weak to even form the words. He realized then that he was leaning against Dan, and had been for the last three hours.

How like Dan that was, Jim managed to think, despite the befuddling haze of pain he was in. Dan, who was himself wounded, had provided a cushion against the bumps of the wagon so that Jim could be as comfortable as possible.

Though it was still dark, there were some who were already up for the morning, and the marshals could see squares of golden light splashing out onto the street, cast there through the windows of the houses where early risers were beginning to sit down to breakfast.

Ned halted them when they reached the end of the street.

"What is it, Ned?" Dan asked.

"That's Doc Urban's house down there," Ned said, pointing to a low, single-story building that sat nearly half a block away from the others. A wisp of wood smoke rose from the chimney, carrying with it the aroma of frying bacon. "Looks like he's already up." Dan clicked to the team, and the wagon slowly covered the remaining distance. They stopped just in front of the doctor's house.

sam urban, m.d., the sign by the door read. Dan carried Jim, and Ned knocked on the door. A moment later it was opened by a short, gray-headed man.

"Ned Remington," he said, recognizing the intruder. He looked around Ned and saw Dan, himself wounded, Standing there with Jim. "Get him in, quickly," he ordered. "Get him over there to the bed."

A pretty young woman was standing at the wood stove, frying bacon. She looked around as Ned and Dan maneuvered Jim over to the bed. Self-consciously, the girl clutched at the neck of her housecoat. She needn't have been concerned, the housecoat preserved as much modesty as if it had been a day dress.

"My daughter, Clara," Urban introduced. "She can assist me."

"I don't know, Doc. He's shot in a pretty delicate place," Ned said as they lay Jim out on the bed. "What do you mean, 'delicate'?"

"What he means is, I'm shot in the butt," Jim explained. "Near 'bout, anyway. Do you think it's seemly for the girl . . ." He let the question hang.

"Don't worry about my daughter. She's assisted me before. Besides there's no such thing as a delicate place as far as a bullet is concerned," Urban said. "Clara, bring a pan of hot water."

"I've biscuits, eggs, and bacon," Clara said as she stepped away from the stove, carrying the pan of water her father asked for. "You men help yourselves. It'll just get cold otherwise."

"Thanks," Ned said. He walked over to the sideboy and picked up a hot, fluffy biscuit.

"Are you in a great deal of pain?" Urban asked as he opened his bag and began putting surgeon's instruments on a bedside table.

"Not as bad as it was," Jim answered.

"I suspect it's a little numb now," Doc Urban said. "It'll wake up when I start probing, though, so I better give you somethin' for it. Here's a little laudanum," Urban said, handing Jim a small vial. "Take it, then drop your pants and turn over so I can get to the wound."

Jim took one look at Clara, then, with no further question, he dropped his trousers. A moment later his under drawers came down, and he turned to lie on his side. Clara bathed the ugly red and black wound on his hip with the warm water she had brought to the table.

With Clara holding a lantern and handing him his probes and forceps, Urban began digging into the wound for the bullet. Ned and Dan were concerned for their friend, but they were also hungry. The breakfast was too good to pass up, so they ate while the operation went on. A few minutes later, Urban announced that he had the bullet and dropped it with a clink into the pan of water. A small curl of blood bubbled to the surface of the water. Clara packed the wound with medicinal salve and began applying the bandage.

"Now, what about you?" Urban asked, looking over at Dan.

"It is nothing. The arrow is out."

"Then let me clean and dress it so that it stays nothing," Urban suggested.

With a shrug, Dan took off his shirt and sat quietly while Dr. Urban removed the old, dirty bandage Ned had made with the torn shirttail. He cleaned the wound, packed it, then dressed it with a new bandage.

"Half the men who die of gunshot wounds would never die if they just knew to keep their wounds clean," Urban complained. "I don't know what's in dirt to cause a wound to mortify, but there must be something."

"Thanks for taking care of us, Doc," Ned said.

"Glad to help. The German said you would be in today."

"You've met Kurt?"

"No, not exactly. I did examine some of his handiwork last night, though."

"What do you mean?"

"There was a shooting fracas. Our sheriff was killed, and your man killed the hombre that shot our sheriff."

"What was it about?"

"It must've been a play to get the Indian out of jail. By the time your deputy got back to the jail, there was someone out back, trying to get the Indian out. Your man drove him off."

"Luckless," Ned said. "He must've figured out where we were going and beat us here."

"You think he'll try again?" Doc Urban asked.

"I'm sure of it," Ned answered. "Listen, I'm sorry about your sheriff. I'm sorry he got caught up in it."

"It was his job," Doc Urban said. "I don't think he would've wanted it any other way. You might have some trouble with the town board, though. They're pretty hot about having the Indian here. They're afraid it's going to turn the town into a battleground."

"They may be right," Ned said solemnly. "But if so, we'll keep it under control as much as possible."

"What about these two? Were they shot when you captured the Indian?"

"Not when we captured him. But a bunch of Comanches jumped us to try to get Tom Blue free."

"I hope you made them pay for the wounds they gave you," Urban said.

"We killed ten of them," Ned said.

"Ten? My God, you've declared war on the Comanches all by yourself."

"I hope not," Ned said. "I hope, and believe, they were all rogues, just like Tom Blue. And if that's the case, the good Indians will be just as happy to see their kind go as the white people will."

"But someone wants him free."

"Yes, a handful of lawbreakers, white and Indian."

"Is it true, what they're telling down at the saloon? Is the only warrant you have for Tom Blue for thieving?"

"That's right."

"You know damn well he's done a lot more than that."

"I know it."

"What are you going to do with him when you get him back?"

"Hang him," Ned said simply.

"For thieving?"

"What difference does it make what we hang him for? Dead is dead. I don't think we'll have any trouble making murder cases against him, but even if we can't, if the only thing we seem able to pin on him is thievin', then by God we'll hang him for that."

"What makes you think a court would go along with that?" Doc Urban wanted to know.

Ned chuckled. "Doc, this is Judge Barnstall's court. He does pretty much what he damn pleases. If he wants to hang Tom Blue for spitting on the streets, that's what he'll do. He has the authority. It comes from the President in Washington."

"I've heard Judge Barnstall is a tough one. What about the Indian? Do you think he knows what's in store for him?"

"He knows," Ned said.

"I guess that's why his friends are trying so hard to get him out. Do you think they'll try to take him out of the town, or will they wait until you are on the road again?" Doc Urban asked.

"I think they'll come here," Ned said. "With your sheriff dead, I guess I'll have to work with the deputy. How is he? Will he help?"

"Angus Conn? Well, yes, I guess he'll do what he can," Doc Urban said. "He seems like a good man. He's young, he doesn't have any experience, but Sheriff Epperson seemed to like him." Doc Urban chuckled.

"What is it?"

"After Epperson was killed, Mayfield and McKenzie—they're two members of the town board—tried to bully Angus into turning out your prisoner. I guess they thought with Epperson gone they'd have a pushover. Anyway, from what I understand, Angus stood up to them. The town board won't hire any extra deputies or anything like that, but I reckon you can count on Angus for help, if need be."

"Good, good. I don't want any extra deputies anyway. They just get in the way," Ned said. "I'd rather go it with a few good men than try to tell them what to do. I'll use Angus to keep a lid on the rest of the town while my deputies and I take care of whatever Mr. Luckless might have in store. Now, what about Jim? Will he be able to help?"

Urban looked over at Jim, who was reclining on the bed.

"Give him a few hours' rest," Urban said. "If the fever has gone down in his leg by then, he'll be all right."

"I'll be with you," Jim mumbled, surprising Ned, who thought he was asleep. "Don't open the ball without me."

Chapter 15

GUTHRIE WAS ALIVE with excitement the next morning. The gunfight at the livery stable grew with each telling.

"I'm tellin' you, I was that close I could hear the primers snap and smell the gunpowder. They stood there, the marshal and the sheriff on one side, Poke Patterson and Grady Martin on the other. 'Throw up your hands,' the sheriff called an' Grady, he says, 'You'll never get me alive!' and he commenced a'firin'."

"It weren't no such thing," another insisted. "They come right out onto the street, all four of 'em, with their guns in their holsters. 'Go for it!' Grady yells, an' all of 'em commenced their draw at about the same time. Poke, he shot the sheriff, an' the marshal shot Grady. Now, that's the way it was."

By the afternoon telling of the story, there were few, even among those who had witnessed the events at the livery stable, who could really tell anymore what actually happened.

In addition to the gunfight at the livery stable there was more excitement to talk about. Three more U.S. Marshals had arrived in town in the middle of the night, driving a black jail wagon. They went straight to Doc Urban's house. It was said that the marshals and Comanches had a gun battle out on the prairie. Ten Comanches were killed, but two of the marshals were wounded, one of whom was dying. Some said he had already died but they were keeping it a secret so the Comanches wouldn't find out about it.

There was one thing everyone agreed upon. The combination of the gunfight last night, the fight on the prairie, and the jailing of Comanche Tom Blue, managed to make Guthrie an exciting place. People poured into town from miles around just to talk about the events and to speculate on whether or not the Comanches would try to rescue Tom Blue. As a result of all this interest, business was never better. The hotel was full, the saloon was busy, and Loomis McKenzie did a greater one-day volume of trade than he had ever done before. He felt a sense of obligation to Sheriff Epperson for making it all possible, so he made a special point of going down to the jail to tell Angus Conn about it.

''I have to tell you, Angus, you an' the sheriff were right an' I was wrong. It is a good thing to have Tom Blue in our jail. It's good for the town.''

"You mean good for business, don't you?" Angus asked.

"Well, yes. But what's good for business is good for the town. And to think I wanted Tom Blue moved out last night. If he had been moved, there wouldn't have been an attempt to rescue him an' we wouldn't be having the business like we're having today."

"And Sheriff Epperson would be alive."

"I suppose so," McKenzie said. "But who knows about a thing like that? He could have stepped out in the road an' been hit by a runaway wagon. Anyway he's dead an' there's no sense crying over spilt milk. You're the new sheriff now, an' I want you to know that Mayfield an' I will back you every step of the way."

"Thanks," Angus said.

"Say, you know what would really be good? If we could hang him here, right in the middle of town. That would really be something, wouldn't it?"

"I don't know. Why don't you ask Tom Blue what he thinks about that?" Angus said. "How about it, Tom Blue? Would you like to hang here?"

"Look at him. He's not talking much, is he?" McKenzie said. He moved a little closer to the cell. "Guess you're not so tough now, are you, Indian?" Angus stood up and put on his hat. "I'm going to take a walk around town. You want to keep an eye on the prisoner for me?"

"What? Me?" McKenzie gasped. "No, uh, I'm not a sheriff. That's what we pay you for."

Angus chuckled as he stepped out onto the front porch. Though he didn't share it with McKenzie, he realized he was laughing at himself as much as he was laughing at McKenzie, for he had experienced the same degree of fear yesterday when Tom Blue was first left in his charge.

At a small campsite about two miles out of town, Nate Luckless stood on a little hill and looked toward Guthrie, which was shimmering in the distance. Rufus Coyote was back with the news that the jail wagon, just as Luckless had suspected, was now in Guthrie. That meant all four marshals were together again.

There were four marshals, but there were five others beside himself, counting Poke Patterson who had joined their number yesterday. That made it six to four; not as good odds as he would want, but it would have to do. The odds might be better ... he had reason to believe that at least one of the marshals was badly wounded. If he knew for sure, he would feel a lot better.

"Well, hell," Moorhead said as he relieved himself against a shrub, directing his stream against a praying mantis. "The best way to find out iffen one of 'em is hurt is to send somebody in there to look around."

"Who would I send?" Luckless asked. "I can't go, they know what I look like. We sure can't send one of the Comanches, and Poke here just kilt their sheriff and the stable boy."

"I ain't goin'," Butler said quickly. "I used to live here. They's probably a lot folks still know me."

"I'll go," Moorhead said, buttoning his pants.

"I'll go, too," Poke volunteered.

"You can't go, everyone knows you."

"Yeah, but I also know the town," Poke said. "I can sneak aroun', dodge behind the buildin's, go up the alleys. Nobody will see me. Besides, with both of us, we're more likely to get the information you need."

Luckless stroked his beard. "All right," he said. "But if you get caught, it's your funeral. I'm havin' enough trouble tryin' to rescue the damned Indian. I ain't gonna make it worse by tryin' to get you, too."

"Don't you worry about me," Poke said.

"I'll tell you one thing," Moorhead put in. "We ain't goin' in together. I don't want to be seen with you."

Poke laughed. "You'll never even know I'm around," he said.

Frank and Poke waited until dark before they went into town. Poke left with him, but, true to his word, he disappeared into the darkness a few minutes after they left the camp. Moorhead rode the rest of the way to town by himself.

Moorhead stopped just on the edge of town. He looked down the main street of Guthrie. There were lights in several of the houses, most of them dim yellow glows from candles, but some were the brighter coal oil lamps. The brightest lights of all poured through the windows and doors of the town's only saloon.

Moorhead heard a squeal, and he whirled around with his gun drawn, then saw a half dozen kids playing kick-the-can. Sheepishly, he put the gun away. A little farther down the street a man and woman were sitting on a porch bench, enjoying the night air. Farther, still, he could see people going in and out of the saloon, and that was where he headed.

Moorhead rode his horse slowly, the hollow, clumping sounds of the hooves bouncing back from the buildings that fronted the street. He stopped in front of the saloon and looped the reins around the hitching rail. Next door to the saloon he saw the jail, and in front of the jail, the wagon they had been following. This was the closest he had gotten to it so he stood there and looked at it for a long moment.

"That's some contraption, ain't it?" a voice said from behind him. The man who spoke was leaning against the front of the saloon. He was about forty-five, paunchy, and unarmed. "It's what they call a Black Maria," the man went on.

"Looks like a jail," Moorhead said.

The paunchy man chuckled. "Well, hell, mister, that's what it is," he said. "Federal marshals take it out into the Nations or out into the territories to bring back prisoners. Put a fella in that, he's just as secure as if he was in a real jail. Fact is, we got Tom Blue in jail right now an' they'll be takin' him up to Missouri in that wagon. That's partly what all the excitement's about in town."

"You don't say," Moorhead said. He stepped up to the bat-wing doors and pushed his way into the saloon. There were at least two dozen people inside, scattered along the bar or sitting at the tables. A handful of painted women moved through the crowd, joking with the men, cajoling some to buy them drinks. Moorhead stepped up to the bar. Though it was diy in the Nations, one could always find a bar in the territory.

"What'll it be, mister?" the bartender asked.

"Beer."

The bartender drew a beer from the barrel, then set it on the bar before him. Moorhead paid for it, then blew the foam off. He thought of Luckless, Butler, and the two Comanches waiting for him outside of town, and he knew how much they would probably appreciate a cool beer. But he felt no sympathy for them. In fact, the idea that he had it and they didn't make the beer taste even better to him, and he drank it down without ever lowering the glass from his lips.

"Another," he said.

The bartender set a second glass before him.

"I don't guess you heard about the excitement," the bartender said.

"What excitement?"

"Why, mister, there was a big gunfight here last night, right in the middle of the street. Our sheriff was killed, and a fine young stable boy. But one of the gunmen, a fella name of Grady Martin, was kilt by a U.S. Deputy Marshal . . . fella by the name of Kurt Hammer. Ever hear tell of him?"

"Can't say as I have."

"You will. He was as fast as lightnin', but, get this: he's just a deputy, an' they say that the fella that's in charge of 'em all, a man name of Ned Remington, is the fastest of them all."

"Is that a fact?"

"Maybe you noticed the Black Maria sitting outside as you came in?"

"Yeah, I seen it."

"Well, sir, there's four marshals come down here with it," the bartender went on, and he told Moorhead the latest version of the story that was making the rounds. By now nearly forty Indians had gone down under the marshals' blazing guns, and no fewer than one hundred were set to msh the town the next day.

"Charlie, you talk too much," the man next to Moorhead said. He was tall, big-boned, young, and he was wearing a badge.

"You one of the deputies he was talking about?"

"I'm a deputy," the man said. "But not a U.S. Deputy Marshal. I'm deputy sheriff for this town. The name's Conn, Angus Conn."

"Angus is the only sheriff we got now," the bartender added quickly.

"I hear tell some of the marshals was shot up pretty bad."

"'Bout dead, they say," the bartender put in quickly.

"I don't believe I caught your name," Angus said. "Moore. Frank Moore," Moorhead said, using the alias he sometimes used.

"Where are you from, Mr. Moore?"

"Up in the Cherokee Strip, a bit the other side of Fort Supply."

Angus had talked to Kurt during the long hours of last night, and he had a pretty good idea of who the marshals were after and where they were from. He had a gut feeling, his first as a lawman, that this was one of the people Marshal Remington and his men were after. He decided to tiy something.

"I used to know a fella up that way, a trader by the name of Luckless. Nate Luckless. You ever run across him?"

"Sure, why Nate an' me we're—" Moorhead started, then he stopped. "That is, I know of him. What's ol' Nate doin' now?"

"I don't know," Angus said. "I haven't heard from him in a long time. Well, it's been nice talking to you, Mr. Moore. I've got to make my rounds. See you around sometime." Angus touched fingers to the brim of his hat and left the saloon.

"You could'a brung a bottle of good whiskey," Luckless complained an hour later when Moorhead returned to the camp to share what information he had found.

"They didn' have no whiskey no better'n the stuff you got," Moorhead said.

"Well, hell, we ain't even got none of that left, the damned Comanches drank it all," Butler said. "I'd'a been satisfied with that."

"I tried to get some, but the bartender said he couldn't sell me no whole bottle. Said it's ag'in the town law," Moorhead lied.

"They sure got strange laws in that town," Butler said.

"Never mind all that. What'd you find out?"

"Looks like they plannin' on movin' Tom Blue tomorrow," Moorhead said. "I seen that they got the Black Maria backed up right in front of the jail, and they ain't no other reason for it but that."

"They got the what backed up there?" Butler asked.

"The Black Maria," Moorhead said.

"What the hell's that?"

"That's what they call the jail wagon," Moorhead explained smugly. "Don't you know nothin'?"

"Go on, go on," Luckless said. "What about the marshals? Was any of 'em hurt like we thought?"

"Yeah," Moorhead said, smiling broadly. "One of 'em's hurt real bad, maybe even dead by now. An' one o' the others is s'posed to be hurt pretty bad, too."

"What about the town? Is there anyone in the town that can help them?"

"No. The sheriff got shot last night an' the only one left is the town deputy. He's a young kid. He won't give us no trouble. Hell, Poke prob'ly knows him. He can tell us about him." Moorhead looked around. "Where is Poke?" he asked.

"I don't know. He ain't come back," Luckless said. "Why not?"

"How the hell am I s'posed to know?" Luckless demanded. "He ain't come back, that's all I know."

"He better not do anythin' to mess us up," Moorhead said. "If he does I'll kill him myself."

Chapter 16

ANGUS TOLD THE MAN in the saloon that he had to make the rounds. In fact, he was just using that as an excuse. He really wanted to get back to the jail and tell Kurt and Dan that someone was in town trying to get information about their plans for moving the prisoner.

"What did he look like?" Kurt wanted to know.

"He was a tall man, skinny, with a large mustache," Angus said. "He said his name was Frank Moore."

"The name doesn't mean anything to me. How about you, Kurt?" Dan asked.

"I don't know the name," Kurt said. "But Laurel described the two men who bought her from the Indians, remember? One of them fits this description."

"Yes," Dan said. "Yes, I think you are right."

"He said he was from the Cherokee Strip," Angus went on.

"That would put him in the right place," Dan suggested.

Angus smiled broadly. "And I tricked him into admitting that he knew Nate Luckless. It wasn't something he wanted to tell me, either. As soon as he admitted it, he started coughing and stammering, then he said he hadn't seen Luckless in a long time."

"What do you think, Kurt? Is Mr. Conn going to make a good lawman?" Dan asked, patting Angus on the back.

"*Ja.* That was a good trick getting him to talk about Luckless."

Angus beamed under the praise. "I just had a feeling," he said. "Sheriff Epperson used to talk about getting a feeling all the time, but I didn't know what he meant. Now I do."

"It comes with the badge," Dan said with a wry grin.

Kurt got up and walked back to the cell to look in at Tom Blue. Though the bunk was handy, the Indian was sitting cross-legged on the floor.

"You heard us talking," he said. "Who was the man Sheriff Conn met in the saloon?"

Tom Blue said nothing, and Kurt smiled and shook his head. "I didn't think you wanted to tell me anything, I was just trying to be friendly, that's all."

"If I say who he is, what you give me?" Tom Blue asked.

Kurt looked over toward the stove and saw the coffeepot. "Right now I couldn't promise you anything more than a cup of coffee," he said. "I guess you wouldn't want to sell out a friend for a cup of coffee."

"Beer?" Tom Blue asked.

Kurt smiled and looked over at Angus. "Go next door and get our guest a beer," he said.

A moment later Tom Blue turned the glass of beer up to his lips and took a long swallow. Kurt, remembering how good the beer had tasted to him after the long ride into Guthrie, and realizing that this was the first taste Tom Blue had had since he was captured, felt almost sorry for his prisoner. Then he thought of his cousin Chris Doomey and his family and workers, and he thought of Clyde Miller and Laurel's mother, father, and sister, and he thought of Linus Rawlings. The sympathy he felt didn't last very long.

"All right, who was it?" he asked.

"His name is Frank Moorhead," Tom Blue said.

"Is he the one who paid you for the girl?"

"Yes," Tom Blue said. "Frank Moorhead and Willis Butler. The girl thought they came to save her because they were white." He leered. "When the white men were through with her, she begged for me to take her back."

Kurt looked at the Indian for a long moment, and he was so filled with disgust and hate that he had to turn his back to the cell to fight against the urge to shoot him. He walked over to sit beside Dan and Angus and was quiet for a long moment.

"Are you all right, Kurt?" Dan asked.

"Ja," Kurt said. He looked back toward the cell. Tom Blue was finished with his beer, and he was sitting in the cross-legged position again. "I will be glad to watch him hang," he said.

"Now that I know everything he has done, I wish I could watch it," Angus said.

Dan stood up and stretched. "I think I will take a walk around town. Angus, you want me to check doors and windows for you?"

"Sure, if you don't mind. Do you know what to do?"

Dan smiled. "I was a town marshal before you were in long pants," he said. "It will remind me of old times."

Dan had nearly circled the entire town when he saw something in one of the alleys. He hadn't" been looking directly at the alley, but he caught some movement from the corner of his eye. He made no indication that he had seen anything out of the ordinary, he just continued on by the alley opening. Then, two steps beyond the alley, he pulled his gun and jumped back into the black maw, pressing himself flat against the side of the building. He looked down to the end of the alley and saw a man standing back in the shadows. Dan cocked his pistol, the metallic rolling of the cylinder sounding exceptionally loud in the quiet of the night.

"All right, mister, come out here," he called.

"That you, Angus?"

"No. I'm Marshal Norling," Dan said. "Who are you?"

The man stepped out of the shadows, buttoning his trousers.

"My name's Eddie Clayton," he said. "I'm sorry about stayin' in the shadows like I done, but I was takin' a leak an' didn't want to do it in public. Then when you come in here with a gun drawed on me like that, why, I didn't know what to think, what with all the shootin' and what-all that's been goin' on around here."

Although the man never did come fully out of the shadows, he came far enough for Dan to see that his pistol was in his holster and that he didn't seem to be a threat.

"What'd you say your name was?"

"Clayton, Eddie Clayton," the man said. "You can ask Angus about me. He knows who I am."

With a sigh, Dan let the hammer down on his gun, then slipped it back into his holster. "It's all right," he said. "But at times like this, you'd be better off using a privy and staying out of the shadows."

"Whatever you say, Marshal," the man said, putting his arms down and hurrying off. "Good night," he called.

Dan finished the rounds, then went back to the jail house. He got himself a cup of water from the barrel, then sat down across the desk from Angus.

"I almost shot one of your friends a few moments ago."

"Oh? How?"

"He was taking a leak in the alley," Dan said. "He said his name was Eddie Clayton."

Angus laughed. "I reckon he's come up in the world. Most of the time when he's drunk he'll piss right out on the street. He was the first arrest I ever had in this town. Matter of fact, he sometimes gets drunk and turns himself in, just because he's too drunk and too tired to find his way back out to his place. Of course, I can't really blame him. He lives eight miles from here, and that's a long ride for someone as old as he is."

The hair shot up on Dan's neck and arms, and he sat up straight. "Did you say old?"

"Yes. He's seventy if he's a day."

"Not this man," Dan said. "He was late twenties, maybe early thirties, about five nine, one hundred and forty pounds, black hair, beard and mustache."

"Poke Patterson," Kurt said quickly. He looked at Angus. "Remember? That was your description of him."

"Yes," Angus answered. "What's he doin' back in town?"

"Maybe he was with Moorhead," Kurt suggested. "Maybe he's trying to get an idea on how they can get Tom Blue out of here tomorrow."

Dan moved his chair to the back door. "Let him try tomorrow," he said. "I'm going to stay right here and make certain he doesn't try anything tonight."

Clara fixed a good supper for the marshals and they ate heartily. Then Dan and Kurt excused themselves to go to the jail to help Angus guard Tom Blue. Doc took another look at Jim, then he went out to make the nightly rounds of his sick patients. That left only Ned, Jim, and Clara at Doc Urban's house.

Jim had slept most of the day and was sleeping tonight, snoring lightly. Earlier, Doc Urban had told Ned he was pleased with how well Jim's wound was healing. The twenty-four hours' sleep would go a long way toward restoring him to near full strength, Doc Urban said. Ned remarked, dryly, that twenty-four hours of sleep would do wonders for them all.

After Doc left, Ned spread some paper out on the table and disassembled his Colt .44. He lay the pieces out before him. Very meticulously he began to clean and oil each part of the pistol. There was no conversation for several moments as Ned was engrossed with his revolver and Clara with the dishes. The only sounds were the measured ticking of a grandfather clock, which stood against the wall of the living room, and Jim's rhythmic breathing. In addition, there was an occasional clink or tinkle from Clara's dishpan, as well as the sink of parts being separated or put together as Ned worked. Finally, Clara finished the dishes, folded her dishcloth and towel, then walked over to the stove, where a pot of coffee remained from supper.

"You certainly take good care of that gun," Clara said. She retrieved two cups and poured coffee for each of them. "Would you like a piece of apple pie?"

"Um, no thanks," Ned said, smiling. "If you remember, I ate two pieces at supper."

"I remember," Clara said. She watched him run a cloth through the barrel. "You treat that gun as if . . . " She let the sentence hang.

"As if what?"

"I don't know, almost as if it were something sacred."

"No, not sacred," Ned said. "But I noticed that you cleaned the doc's instruments after he got finished with Jim," Ned said.

"Of course," Clara answered. "They are the tools of his profession."

Ned smiled and pointed to the disassembled pistol. "And this is the tool of my profession."

"Why do you do it?"

"Why am I a peace officer, you mean?"

"Yes. There must be other jobs you could do . . . jobs that wouldn't require you to kill or be killed." Ned paused for a moment and looked at her. "How old are you, Clara?"

"I'm twenty-one."

"Has it been a happy twenty-one years?"

"Yes, I would have to say so," Clara answered. "Except for when my mama died four years ago."

"I do it so your next twenty-one years will be as happy as your first," he said.

"I don't understand."

"You heard us talking about the girl, Laurel, earlier. About how her family was killed and she was captured?"

"Yes."

"There are evil men who prey on people like that, innocent people who want only to live their own lives and be happy. An innocent person is like a lamb among wolves . . . they need someone to protect them, to run the wolves off. Sometimes a wolf can only be run off by another wolf, one who has fangs just as long and just as sharp and who is willing to use them."

"And you are such a wolf?" Clara asked.

"When I have to be."

"But you and Jim, Kurt, and Dan, you are such gentlemen. I can't imagine any of you being like you say."

Suddenly the back door to the house was kicked open, and Ned and Clara looked up to see a man standing there, holding a pistol in front of him.

"Poke Patterson! What are you doing here? Why did you kick our door in like that? Papa isn't here."

"He isn't here for the doctor," Ned said.

Poke looked at Ned and smiled. "You got that right," he said.

"What do you want?" Ned asked.

"They tell me you got yourself quite a reputation, Marshal Remington," he said. He cocked his pistol. "I figure Nate Luckless will pay me pretty good to get rid of you. And I aim to pick up a reputation at the same time. Folks want to buy my gun from now on, they'll be payin' a pretty price for it."

"You think it's going to be all that easy, do you?" Ned asked.

Poke looked at Ned's disassembled pistol on the table. His smile grew broader.

"Well, now, with your gun in pieces there on the table, what do you think?" He cocked his pistol.

"No!" Clara shouted. She stepped in front of Ned.

"Clara, get out of the way," Ned hissed.

"No. He won't kill a woman," Clara insisted.

Poke hesitated for just an instant, then he aimed his pistol at Clara's head.

"Girl, iffen you think I won't kill you, you're full of applesauce," he said.

At that moment Clara got a glimpse of her own mortality. She knew she had miscalculated Poke's intentions. She knew she was about to die.

Jim Early had slept all day long, and now he was drifting in and out. He had heard the soft, droning tones of Ned and Clara while they were talking, and they were soothing to him. Now there was a third voice, a harsh, guttural voice that grated on him and brought him to full wakefulness. Without moving he turned his eyes in the direction of the voice and saw a man holding a pistol on Ned and Clara. He didn't know who the man was, and it didn't matter. He read the expression in the man's eyes, and he knew that he intended to kill.

Jim reached for his pistol, then realized that he wasn't wearing a gun. In fact, he was wearing damn near nothing.

Desperately, he looked around then saw, on the table beside the bed, the scissors Clara had used to make the bandage. Slowly, quietly, he reached for the scissors. He wrapped his fingers around the point then sat up, moving as slowly as he possibly could so that the bedsprings wouldn't creak. When he was in the full upright position, he raised his arm above his head. Then, just as the intruder started to tighten his finger on the trigger, Jim threw the scissors, snapping his wrist forward.

The scissors flew across the room, tumbled once, then buried themselves in the gunman's neck. Poke's hand flew up, and he fired off a round, which whistled by Ned and Clara's heads to crash through the front window. Poke let out a choking gasp, dropped his gun, and grabbed at the scissors with both hands, trying to pull them out. He succeeded in jerking the scissors out of his neck, but when he did so a fountain of blood gushed forth. He fell to his knees, looked toward Jim in surprise, then pitched forward on his face.

Clara turned away from him, and Ned put his arms around her, holding her tightly to him. Ned looked over at Jim.

"It's about time you woke up," he said.

"I told you not to start the ball without me," Jim replied.

Chapter 17

NATE LUCKLESS AND HIS BAND rode into Guthrie at first light the next morning. The main street, the place of so much activity last night, was now deserted. Not a creature was moving, not a human, horse, or dog. It was a quiet that hung in the still air like a graveyard silence.

"I never seen anyplace this quiet before," Willis observed. "It plumb gives me the williwaws."

The two Comanches kept twisting from side to side on their horses, looking at the roofs and into the windows of the houses and stores.

"You sure there's folks livin' in this town?" Willis asked.

"You should'a seen it last night," Frank said. "It was booming like a town fair."

"Oh, sweet Jesus!" Willis suddenly shouted. His outburst was so sudden and unexpected that the horses shied and danced sideways, and the riders had to jerk on the reins to control them.

"What is it?" Luckless asked angrily. "What the hell are you yelling about?"

"Look! Over there in the window of the hardware store!"

When the others looked where Willis directed, they saw a coffin. The top half of the coffin was open, and it was placed at an angle so people who passed by on the street could see it. There was a body in the coffin, dressed in a black suit, white shirt, and black tie. A scarf was around the neck. The face was pasty white with the undertaker's powder. Both eyes were open but one had drooped to a half close. There was a glassiness to the eyes.

"Well, now we know what happened to Poke last night," Luckless said.

The five men rode on down the quiet street. They saw the Black Maria parked in front of the jail, and they rode by it slowly, looking in. The wagon was empty. They went on by the jail to the saloon, then they dismounted.

"Take the horses 'round back," Luckless ordered. "Billy Blackhat, Rufus Coyote, you two get across the street and keep a watch from there. We'll wait in the saloon."

"The saloon ain't open," Frank noticed.

"We'll wait a few minutes," Luckless said. "If it don't open pretty damned quick, we'll open it."

Charlie Anderson lived in one of the houses at the edge of town. He could have lived in an apartment over the saloon, but his wife didn't think it was a fitting place to raise their two kids, so Charlie built a little frame house soon after they moved to Guthrie.

Charlie was making a good living out of the Stock- well Saloon. Most of his customers thought he owned the saloon outright; very few knew that Loomis McKenzie was not only his silent, but also his majority, partner. McKenzie wanted his participation kept secret because there were some who thought all of the territory, and not just the Nations, should be dry. If those people knew that Loomis McKenzie had an interest in a saloon, they might not patronize his mercantile store.

It was just after seven in the morning when Charlie left his house to walk down to the saloon. Three or four shopkeepers were already out, sweeping the porches and walks in front of their places, and they all nodded or spoke to Charlie. He passed by McKenzie's Mercantile.

"How was business last night?" Loomis asked. He was stacking washtubs in front of his store, and he didn't look around. Charlie stopped and struck a sulphur match on the pillar supporting the porch roof, then held it to a cheroot.

"It was pretty fair," he said. "We've never done so much in one day. I figure we'll do even better today; that's why I'm going down to open up early."

"I hope you watered the whiskey."

"I ... I really didn't have time," Charlie said. "We were so busy." Charlie didn't like to water the whiskey, but that was one of the things Loomis insisted upon.

"Make sure you get it done today," Loomis said. He went back into his store, and only the most discerning would realize the two men had been speaking.

Charlie crossed the street, being careful to pick his way around the horse droppings that often had the effect of making the town smell like a barnyard. There were three men waiting on the front porch of the saloon. He recognized one of them from the night before, but he didn't know the other two.

"Good morning, gents," he greeted. "You're getting an early start at it, aren't you?"

"I told them what a fine establishment you ran," the one who had been in the night before said.

"Good, good, a satisfied customer is my best advertisement, I always say." Charlie remembered that Loomis wanted him to water the whiskey and realized that it would take him at least a couple of minutes to get the first few bottles ready. "I'll be open in five minutes, gents," he said.

The big, bearded, bald-headed man pulled his gun and pointed it at Charlie.

"You're gonna let us in now," he hissed. "But you ain't gonna open 'til we tell you."

"What?" Charlie gasped. "Who are you?"

"Nate Luckless. These are my friends Willis Butler and Frank Moorhead." The two with Luckless smiled toothily. "And if you'll look across the street in the alleyway between the laundry and the boot shop, you'll see two more of our friends."

Charlie looked across the street and saw the two Indians.

"Comanches!" he said. "You've come for the prisoner."

"Now you understand," Luckless said. "Open the door."

With trembling hands, Charlie unlocked the front door. A moment later he and the three men stalked inside. Nate closed the door behind him.

The place smelled of its early-morning odor: stale beer and spilt whiskey. The smell was a permanent part of the saloon, and on those rare occasions when his wife came to the place, she complained of it. Charlie seldom noticed it, and at any rate it was generally gone by the middle of the day, washed away by the reek of sweat and smoke.

Luckless checked the *closed* sign in the window to make certain it was facing toward the street, then he pulled up a chair and started watching the wagon and the jail next door.

"How long are you gents going to stay?" Charlie asked in a frightened voice.

"As long as it takes," Luckless replied in a guttural voice. "Bring me a bottle of whiskey."

"Sure," Charlie said. "Sure thing. And it's on the house, too. You don't have to pay a cent."

Luckless chuckled, a quiet, evil chuckle. "Now, ain't that Christian of this fella?" he asked Frank and Willis. "This bottle don't cost us nothin'." He pulled the cork with his teeth, then spit it out on the floor. He turned the bottle up and took several Adam's-apple-bobbing swallows before pulling it down again. The whiskey, which had been high up in the neck of the bottle, was now below the shoulder. He passed the bottle to Willis.

"They're in the saloon," Jim said. Jim Early stood by the front door of the jail, looking out on the street. He was leaning on a cane Doc Urban gave him. Doc assured him that he would only need the cane for a couple of weeks.

Behind Jim, sitting around the sheriff's desk, were Dan, Kurt, and Ned. Standing by the cell was Angus Conn, while Tom Blue sat on the iron cot inside.

"All right," Ned said. "Does everyone know what to do?"

"Ja," Kurt said. "Dan and I will put Tom Blue in the false bottom we've rigged in the Black Maria, then we will get inside."

"I know the sonsofbitches are dumb," Jim said, "but are they dumb enough to fall for the same trick twice? This is what we got them on the last time."

"Not really," Dan said.

"What do you mean?"

"Everyone who fell for it before is dead. We killed them all."

"Yeah," Jim said quietly. "Yeah, I guess you're right."

"Remember, men, I want Luckless alive if we can get him alive," Ned said. "But don't let him get away. I'd rather have the sonofabitch dead than let him light a shuck."

"He won't get away," Jim promised. "I know I ain't gonna participate in your little shindig out there, but I can still shoot, and I'm gonna stand right here and keep an eye on everything. If he looks like he's hightailing it, I'll drop him."

"Angus, the two Comanches are yours," Ned said.

"Right," Angus replied.

"Now, unlock the cell door. We're ready."

"Hey, Nate, you better come over here," Frank called.

Luckless hurried back to the front window and looked next door. He saw Remington coming out of the jail. He had Tom Blue with him.

"When he opens that wagon door, we jump him," Luckless said. He looked across the street beside the laundry and saw the two Comanches. He held up his hand to get their attention, then waited to give the signal.

Meanwhile, Dan and Kurt came out of the jail to flank Ned and the prisoner. Unbeknownst to Luckless and his men, Ned opened the door to the Black Maria, raised the false bottom, and forced Tom Blue down inside. Dan and Kurt got into the back. Ned closed the door, but he didn't lock it.

"That's it," Luckless shouted. He and his two men came storming out of the saloon, and the Comanches rushed across the street. Ned took cover behind the wagon, while Angus ran out of the jail and dived for the cover of the watering trough.

With guns blazing, Frank Moorhead and Willis Butler ran to the Black Maria. They jerked the door open, thinking to rescue Tom Blue. Instead, they found themselves face to face with Dan and Kurt. There was an exchange of almost point-blank gunfire. Bullets crashed into the floor and ceiling of the wagon, but not one of the outlaws' bullets found their mark.

Dan and Kurt, on the other hand, were much more accurate with their shooting. Frank was hit in the neck, shoulder, and twice in the heart. Willis caught bullets in the cheek, right arm, two in the lungs, and one in the heart. Both outlaws were dead before they hit the ground. Their guns lay silent in the dirt.

The Comanches hadn't fired a shot. When they got halfway across the road and saw the withering fire open up from inside the Black Maria, they remembered what just two men had done from this devil wagon when nine of their fellow warriors had been cut down. They didn't Want any part of it, and they skidded to a stop, threw down their guns, and raised their hands. Angus stood up from the watering trough and captured them at gunpoint.

Like many a gunman, Nate Luckless kept only five chambers of his pistol charged. The sixth chamber was left unloaded as a precaution against the pistol going off accidentally. As a result of his wild and ineffective firing, Luckless was soon out of ammunition, with no way or time to reload. As soon as he realized his situation, he started running toward the horses.

Ned saw what was happening and went after him. Ned had the angle on him, and he climbed onto the side rail, then leaped onto him. He and Luckless rolled in the dirt, and Luckless came out on top. With a yell of triumph, Luckless drew back a fist to hit Ned, but Ned rolled out from under him, then jumped to his feet. Luckless got up and turned to face him.

"So, you're going to take me on bare-handed," Luckless said. He smiled. "Anytime, mister. Anytime."

Luckless lowered his head and charged, bull-like, toward Ned. Ned jumped to one side at the last second, then sent a quick left jab aimed at Luckless' head. He was rewarded a moment later when Luckless turned to look at him, still smiling his evil smile, but now with blood trailing across his teeth and matting in his beard. Luckless charged again, and again Ned skipped out of his way, countering with another left jab.

Finally, Luckless decided to stand up to him, and he waded toward Ned, swinging roundhouse rights and lefts. One of them caught Ned on the shoulder, just a glancing blow, and Ned's entire arm went momentarily numb. That's when he realized how strong Nate Luckless really was. It had been only the big man's clumsiness and ineptness that had made it easy for Ned.

By now several people had gathered around to watch the fight, and Ned didn't want that because the more people there were, the better the chance Luckless would have to get away. He had to put the big man down, so he feinted once with his left to pull the man's guard away, and that gave him the opening he needed. He sent a whistling right hand, with everything he had, directly toward Nate Luckless's Adam's apple. He caught it square, felt it crumple to mush under his blow, saw the big man turn blue, then drop to his knees, clutching his neck. A crossing right smash to the point of Nate's chin finished him off, then Kurt and Dan dragged his unconscious form to the back of the Black Maria, where they threw him in with Tom Blue.

A large banner stretched across the street from Grant's Confectionary to Markham's Cafe. The sign read:

GOOD-BYE, MARSHALS REMINGTON, EARLY, NORLING, AND HAMMER. COME TO GUTHRIE AGAIN SOMETIME!

A band stood in formation near the kiosk and, as the Black Maria rolled past, broke into a stirring rendition of "Buffalo Gals." It was the last stage of a day-long celebration to mark the capture of Tom Blue and Nate Luckless. The cap would occur at five that afternoon when outlaws Poke Patterson, Frank Moorhead, and Willis Butler would be buried in the town cemetery, followed by the swearing in of Angus Conn as the new sheriff.

Angus rode alongside the Black Maria, taking his share of waves and greetings from the folks gathered on both sides of the road.

"I guess congratulations are in order," Ned said.

"Not as much in order as thanks," Angus said. "I appreciate you having enough faith in me to use me."

"Sheriff Epperson had faith in you, that was enough for us," Ned said.

"I hope I'm worthy of the job."

"You will be," Kurt said, laughing. "If not, I'll personally come back and tan your hide."

Angus looked into the back of the Black Maria at the sullen faces of Tom Blue and Nate Luckless.

"I guess they aren't enjoying the festivities," he said.

"We've got a special celebration planned for those two," Ned said. "A special event, without regard to race, creed, or color; a hangman is waiting for a white man and an Indian who broke the law and got caught at it."

Justice, thought Ned. It was a sweet word. Almost as sweet a word as *home.*

Remington sat up straight in the saddle and touched spurs to his horse's flanks. "Come on, boy," he said to the gelding. "Let's go home."

THE END

A Look at Long Road to Abilene by Robert Vaughan

Long Road to Abilene, is a classic hero's journey, a western adventure that exemplifies the struggles, the defeats, and the victories that personify the history of the American West. After surviving the bloody battle of Franklin and the hell of a Yankee prison camp, Cade McCall comes home to the woman he loves only to find that she, believing him dead, has married his brother. With nothing left to keep him in Tennessee, Cade journeys to New Orleans where an encounter with a beautiful woman leads to being shanghaied for an unexpected adventure at sea. Returning to Texas, he signs on to drive a herd of cattle to Abilene, where he is drawn into a classic showdown of good versus evil, and a surprising reunion with an old enemy.

Available from Wolfpack Publishing and Robert Vaughan.

About the Author

Robert Vaughan sold his first book when he was 19. That was 57 years and nearly 500 books ago. He wrote the novelization for the mini series *Andersonville*. Vaughan wrote, produced, and appeared in the History Channel documentary Vietnam Homecoming. His books have hit the NYT bestseller list seven times. He has won the Spur Award, the PORGIE Award (Best Paperback Original), the Western Fictioneers Lifetime Achievement Award, received the Readwest President's Award for Excellence in Western Fiction, is a member of the American Writers Hall of Fame and is a Pulitzer Prize nominee. Vaughn is also a retired army officer, helicopter pilot with three tours in Vietnam. And received the Distinguished Flying Cross, the Purple Heart, The Bronze Star with three oak leaf clusters, the Air Medal for valor with 35 oak leaf clusters, the Army Commendation Medal, the Meritorious Service Medal, and the Vietnamese Cross of Gallantry.

Find more great titles by Robert Vaughan and Wolfpack Publishing at http://wolfpackpublishing.com/robert-vaughan/

71208296R00080

Made in the USA
Middletown, DE
20 April 2018